"And now we come to Andreas and Sienna. I think we should conduct this in private. Just the two of you, if the others don't mind."

Andreas felt his spine tighten. He didn't want his name bracketed with that little wildcat. It made him feel edgy. It had always made him feel that way. She was a tearaway who rocked his world in ways he didn't want.

Had never wanted.

He had stayed away from the family home because of her. Sienna's outrageous deceit had destroyed any chance of a working relationship with his father for the past eight years. Andreas blamed her for it all.

He hated her with a vengeance.

The lawyer waited for the others to leave the library before he opened the folder in front of him. "The Chatcau De Chalvy in Provence is entailed to you both, but on the proviso that you live together legally as man and wife for the minimum of six months."

The Outrageous Sisters
The twin sisters everyone's *talking about!*

Separated by secrets…
Growing up in different families, Gisele's and
Sienna's lives are worlds apart. Then a very public
revelation propels them into the world's eye.…

Drawn together by scandal!

Now the sisters have found each other—
but are they at risk of losing their hearts to the
two men who are determined to peel back the
layers of their glittering facade?

Last month Gisele found out if she really was

DERSERVING OF HIS DIAMONDS?

This month read the shocking conclusion in
Sienna's story,

ENEMIES AT THE ALTAR

Melanie Milburne

ENEMIES AT THE ALTAR

HARLEQUIN®

entertain, enrich, inspire™

Recycling programs
for this product may
not exist in your area.

ISBN-13: 978-0-373-23856-9

ENEMIES AT THE ALTAR

Copyright © 2012 by Melanie Milburne

www.Harlequin.com

Printed in U.S.A.

All about the author...
Melanie Milburne

From as soon as **MELANIE MILBURNE** could pick
up a pen she knew she wanted to write. It was when
she picked up her first Harlequin Mills & Boon at
seventeen that she realised she wanted to write romance.
Distracted for a few years by meeting and marrying her
own handsome hero, surgeon husband Steve, and having
two boys, plus completing a masters degree in education
and becoming a nationally ranked athlete (masters
swimming) she decided to write. Five submissions later
she sold her first book and is now a multi-published,
award-winning, *USA TODAY* bestselling author. In
2008 she won the Australian Readers' Association's most
popular category/series romance, and in 2011 she won a
prestigious Romance Writers of Australia R*BY award.

Melanie loves to hear from her readers via her website,
www.melaniemilburne.com.au, or on Facebook.

Other titles by Melanie Milburne available in eBook:

Harlequin Presents®

To my niece Angie Fouche,
who is a beautiful and brave young woman.
Love you. p.s. EEEE!!!!

CHAPTER ONE

ANDREAS got the call from his younger sister Miette in the early hours of the morning.

'Papà is dead.'

Three words that under normal circumstances should have evoked a maelstrom of emotion, but to Andreas they meant nothing other than he was now free from having to play happy families on the extremely rare occasions his path crossed with his father. 'When is the funeral?' he asked.

'Thursday,' Miette said. 'Will you come?'

Andreas glanced at the sleeping woman lying beside him in the king-sized hotel bed. He rubbed at his stubbled jaw and let out a frustrated sigh. It was just typical of his father to choose the most inconvenient time to die. This coming weekend in Washington DC was where he had planned to ask Portia Briscoe to marry him once his business here was complete. He even had the ring in his briefcase. Now he would have to wait for another opportunity to propose. There was no way he wanted his engagement and marriage to be forever associated with anything to do with his father, even his demise.

'Andreas?' Miette's voice pierced his reverie and his conscience. 'It would be good if you could be there, for me even if not for Papà. You know how much I hate funerals, especially after Mamma's.'

Andreas felt a claw of anger clench at his insides at the thought of their beautiful mother and how cruelly she had been betrayed. He was sure *that* had been what had finally killed her, not the cancer. The shame of finding out her husband was sleeping with the hired help while she was battling gruelling rounds of chemotherapy had broken her spirit *and* her heart.

And then, to add insult to injury, the brazenness of that witch Nell Baker and her trashy little sleep-around slut of a daughter Sienna had turned his mother's final farewell into a cheap and tawdry soap opera.

'I'll be there,' he said.

But that little hot-headed harlot Sienna Baker had better not.

The first person Sienna saw when she arrived at the funeral in Rome was Andreas Ferrante.

At least her eyes registered it was him, but she had *felt* him seconds earlier in her body. As soon as she had stepped over the portal she had felt a shiver run up her spine and her heart had started a crazy little pitter-patter beat that was nothing like its normal, healthy, steady rhythm.

She hadn't seen him in years and yet she had *known* he was there.

He was sitting in one of the pews at the front of the cathedral. Even though he had his back towards her she could see he was as staggeringly gorgeous as ever. His aristocratic bearing was like an aura that surrounded him. He exuded wealth and power and status. His glossy raven-black head was several inches higher than any of the other black-suited men sitting nearby, his thick, slightly wavy hair neither long nor short, but cut and styled so it brushed against the collar of his shirt.

He turned his head and leaned down to say something to the young woman seated beside him. Just seeing the profile of his face made Sienna want to put a hand to her chest where her heart was flapping like a frantic fish suddenly flung out of its fish tank. For years she had dismissed his features from her mind. She had dared not think of him. He was a part of her past she was ashamed of—*deeply* ashamed. She had been so young and foolish, so immature and insecure. She hadn't thought through the consequences of twisting the truth. But then, who did at the age of seventeen?

And then, as if Andreas sensed her looking at him, he twisted his head and locked gazes with her. It was like a lightning strike when those hazel eyes hit hers. They narrowed and glared, pinning her to the spot like a bug on a corkboard.

Sienna pasted an indifferent smile on her face and, giving her silver-blonde head a toss, sashayed up the aisle and shimmied her way into a pew on the left hand side a few rows back from his.

She *felt* his anger.

She *felt* his rage.

She *felt* his fury.

It made her skin shiver. It made her vertebrae rattle like ice cubes in a glass. It made her blood race. It made her knees feel weak, as if someone had removed all of her strong stabilising ligaments and put overcooked noodles in their place.

But she showed none of that. Instead, she affected a cool poise that her teenage self, eight years ago, would have sorely envied.

The woman seated beside him was his latest mistress, or so Sienna had gathered from a recent press article. Portia Briscoe had lasted longer than any of his other lovers, which made Sienna wonder if the faint whisper she had heard of an impending engagement had any truth to it.

Not that she had ever thought of Andreas Ferrante as the falling in love type. To her he had always been the playboy prince of prosperity and privilege. When the time came he would choose a bride to suit his Old Money heritage. Just like his father and grandfather before him, love would not come into it at all.

Although, going on appearances alone, Portia Briscoe looked like the perfect candidate to be the next generation Ferrante bride. She was classically beautiful in a carefully constructed way. The sort of woman who never went anywhere without perfectly coiffed hair and expertly applied make-up. She was the type of woman who wouldn't dream of turning up at a funeral on a whim, in faded jeans with ragged hems and soiled trainers or, God forbid, a T-shirt that had suffered a food spill.

Portia Briscoe *only* wore exquisitely tailored designer couture. She even had toothpaste commercial teeth and porcelain skin that looked as if it had never suffered a blemish on it.

Unlike Sienna, who'd had to endure the torture of braces for two years and had only that morning had to reach for her concealer to cover a spot on her chin.

Andreas Ferrante would make sure his bride never put a designer-clad foot out of place. His bride wouldn't have a history of bad choices and reckless behaviour that had caused more pain and shame than she cared to think about.

No, his bride would be Perfect Portia, not shameful, scandalous Sienna.

Good luck to him.

As soon as the service was drawing to a close, Sienna slipped out of the church. She still wasn't exactly sure why she had felt compelled to pay her respects to a man in death she hadn't even liked in life. But she had seen the news in the press about his death from a heart attack and immediately thought of her mother.

Her mother Nell had *loved* Guido Ferrante.

Nell had worked for the Ferrante family for years, but not once had Guido acknowledged her as anything but his housekeeper. Sienna remembered all too well the scandal her mother had caused at Evaline Ferrante's funeral. The press had gone wild with it, like a pack of hyenas over a carcass. It had been one of the most humiliating experiences of her life. To see her mother vilified, to see her shamed in the most appalling way, was something Sienna still carried with her. She had sworn that day she would never be at the mercy of a powerful man. *She* would be the one in control. She would be the agent of her own destiny, not have her life dictated to by others who had been better born or had more money than her.

She would *never* fall in love.

'Excuse me, Miss Baker?' A well-dressed man in his late fifties approached. 'Sienna Louise Baker?'

Sienna set her shoulders squarely. 'Who wants to know?' she asked.

The man held out a hand. 'Allow me to introduce myself,' he said. 'I am Lorenzo Di Salle, Guido Ferrante's lawyer.'

Sienna took his hand briefly. 'Nice to meet you. Now, if you'll excuse me, I have to go.'

She had barely moved a step before the lawyer's words stopped her in her tracks. 'You are invited to be at the reading of Guido Ferrante's will.'

Sienna turned back around and stared at him with her mouth open. 'Pardon?'

'As a beneficiary to Signor Ferrante's estate you are—'

'A *beneficiary*?' she gasped. 'But why?'

The lawyer gave her a smile Sienna didn't much care for. 'Signor Ferrante has left some property to you,' he said.

'Property?' she said blankly. 'What property?'

'The Chateau de Chalvy in Provence,' he said.

Sienna's heart did a double shuffle. 'There must be some mistake,' she said. 'That was Evaline Ferrante's family home. Surely it should go to Andreas or Miette?'

'Signor Ferrante insisted it be left to you,' he said. 'There are, however, some conditions attached.'

Sienna narrowed her eyes. 'Conditions?'

Lorenzo Di Salle gave her a serpentine smile. 'The reading of the will is in the library at the Ferrante villa at three p.m. tomorrow. I look forward to seeing you there.'

Andreas prowled the length and breadth of the library feeling like a lion in a cat carrier. He hadn't been to his family home in years, not since the night Sienna had been found all but naked in his bedroom at the age of seventeen. The little she-devil had lied her way out of it, making him out to be some sort of lecher while she had maintained the act of innocent victim, a role she played all too well. Why else had his father included her in his will? She wasn't a blood relative. She was the housekeeper's daughter. She was nothing but a little gold-digging slut who had already married once for money. She had obviously inveigled her way into his ailing father's affections to get her greedy little hands on what she could, now that her elderly husband had died, leaving her practically penniless. His mother's estate in Provence was the one thing Andreas would do anything to keep out of Sienna's possession.

And he meant *anything*.

The door opened and Sienna Baker came breezing in as if she owned the place. At least today she had dressed a little more appropriately, but not by much. Her short denim skirt showed off the long slim length of her coltish sun-kissed legs and her white blouse was tied at her impossibly slender waist, showing a glimpse of the toned flesh of her abdomen. She didn't have a scrap of make-up on her face and her silver-blonde hair was loose around her shoulders, but even so she looked as if she had just stepped off a photo shoot.

The whole room seemed to suck in a breath and hold it. Andreas had seen it happen so many times. Her totally natural beauty was like a punch to the solar plexus. He had worked hard over the years to disguise his reaction, but even now he could feel the effect she had on him. He had felt it yesterday in the church. He had known the very minute she had arrived.

He had *sensed* it.

He glanced at his watch before throwing her a contemptuous glare. 'You're late.'

She gave him a pert look as she flipped her hair over one shoulder. 'It's two minutes past three, Rich Boy,' she said. 'Don't be so anal.'

The lawyer rustled his papers on the desk. 'Could we get started?' he asked. 'There's a lot to go through. Let's start with Miette…'

Andreas remained standing as the will was read out. He was glad his younger sister was well provided for, not that she needed it as she and her husband had a very successful investment business based in London, but it was a relief to know she hadn't been elbowed out by that brazen little blow-in. Miette had inherited the family villa in Rome and assets worth millions set in trust for her two young children. It was a satisfying result given that Miette—like Andreas—hadn't been all that close to their father over the last years of his life.

'And now we come to Andreas and Sienna,' Lorenzo Di Salle said. 'I think we should conduct this part of the reading in private. Just the two of you, if the others don't mind.'

Andreas felt his spine tighten. He didn't want his name bracketed with that little wildcat. It made him feel edgy. It had always made him feel that way. She was a tearaway who rocked his world in ways he didn't want.

Had *never* wanted.

He had stayed away from the family home because of her. For years he hadn't stepped over the threshold, not even to spend those few precious weeks with his mother before she died. Sienna's outrageous deceit had destroyed any chance of a working relationship with his father for the last eight years. Andreas blamed her for it all. She was a sly little vixen intent on her own gain.

He hated her with a vengeance.

The lawyer waited for the others to leave the library before he opened the folder in front of him. 'The Chateau de Chalvy in Provence is entailed to you both but on the proviso that you live together legally as man and wife for the minimum of six months.'

Andreas heard the lawyer's words but it took a moment for them to register. He felt a shockwave go through him. It was like being shoved backwards by a toppling bookcase. He couldn't get his throat unlocked to speak. He stood staring at the lawyer, wondering if he had imagined what he had just heard.

Sienna and him...married.

Legally tied.

Stuck together for six months.

It was a joke.

'This has got to be a joke,' Andreas said, raking a hand through his hair.

'It's no joke,' Lorenzo Di Salle said. 'Your father changed his will in the last month of his life. He was adamant about it. If you don't agree to marry each other within the time frame, the property will be handed over to a distant relative.'

Andreas knew exactly which distant relative the lawyer was referring to. He also knew how quickly his mother's ancestral home would be sold to feed the second cousin's gambling addiction. His father had laid the perfect trap. He had thought of everything, every get out clause and every escape route. He had made it impossible for Andreas to do anything but obey his orders.

'I'm not marrying him!' Sienna shot to her feet, her grey-blue eyes flaring in outrage.

Andreas flicked her a disparaging glance. 'Sit down and shut up, for God's sake.'

She pushed her chin up, her bottom lip going forward in a pout. 'I'm not marrying you.'

'I'm very glad to hear it,' Andreas said dryly and turned to the lawyer. 'There's got to be a way out of this. I'm about to become engaged. You have to make this go away.'

The lawyer lifted his hands in a gesture of defeat. 'The will is iron-clad,' he said. 'If either of you refuses to cooperate, the other automatically inherits everything.'

'What?' Andreas and Sienna spoke at once.

Andreas threw her a look before he addressed the lawyer. 'You mean if I don't agree to marry her she inherits Chateau de Chalvy, plus all the other assets?'

Lorenzo nodded. 'And if you do marry and one of you walks out before the six months is up, the one who stays inherits everything by default,' he said. 'Signor Ferrante set it up so neither of you have a choice but to marry each other and stay married for six months.'

'Why six months?' Sienna asked.

Andreas rolled his eyes as he muttered,

'Because any longer than that he knew I would probably end up on a murder charge.'

Sienna sent him a withering look. 'Only if you got in first.'

Andreas dismissed her comment by turning back to the lawyer. 'What happens at the end of six months if we do decide to stick it out?' he asked.

'You get the chateau and Sienna gets a pay-out,' the lawyer said.

'How big a pay-out?' Sienna asked.

Lorenzo named a sum that sent Andreas's brows sky-high. 'She gets that much for doing what exactly?' he asked. 'Flouncing around pretending to be the lady of the manor for six months? That's outrageous!'

Sienna curled her lip at him. 'I'd say it was pretty fair compensation for having to put up with you for six days, let alone six months.'

Andreas narrowed his eyes to paper-thin slits. 'You put him up to this, didn't you?' he said through clenched teeth. 'You got him to write this crazy will so you could get your greedy little hands on whatever you could.'

Her grey-blue eyes held his defiantly. 'I haven't seen or spoken to your father for five years,' she said. 'He didn't even have the decency to send me a card or flowers when my mother died, let alone attend her funeral.'

Andreas stared her down. 'Why did you come to his funeral if you hated him so much?'

Her chin stayed at a pugnacious height. 'Don't think I would've made a special trip because I damn well wouldn't,' she said. 'I was here for a dress fitting for my sister's wedding next month.'

'I heard about your long lost twin,' Andreas said. 'I read about it in the paper.' He curled his lip and added, 'God help us all if she's anything like you.'

She glared at him furiously. 'I came to your father's funeral out of respect for my mother,' she said. 'She would've come if she was still alive. Nothing on this earth would have stopped her.'

Andreas gave her a mocking look. 'No, not even common decency, it seems.'

She shot to her feet with a hand raised to slap him. He only managed to stop it from connecting with his jaw by grasping her wrist in mid-air. The shock of her soft silky skin against his fingers was like a power surge going through his body. He saw the sudden flare of her eyes as if she had felt it too.

A nanosecond passed.

Something entered the air between them,

a primal, dangerous thing that had no name, no shape or form—*it was just there*.

Andreas dropped her wrist and stepped back from her, surreptitiously opening and closing his fingers to see if they were still able to function. 'You'll have to excuse Miss Baker—' he spoke to the lawyer again '—she has a reputation for histrionics.'

Sienna threw Andreas a filthy look. 'Bastard.'

The lawyer closed the folder and got to his feet. 'You have a week to come to a decision,' he said. 'I suggest you think about this carefully. There's a lot to lose on both sides if you don't cooperate.'

'I've already decided,' Sienna said, folding her arms across her chest. 'I'm not marrying him.'

Andreas laughed. 'Nice try, Sienna,' he said. 'There's no way you'd turn your back on that amount of money.'

She came and stood right in his body space, her chin up, her eyes flashing, her hands on her slim hips, her beautiful breasts heaving. He had never felt such raw sexual energy coming towards him in his life. His whole body jolted with it. It was like being zapped with a Taser gun. He felt it rush through every vein like a flood of roaring fire. His groin pulsated as she leaned in closer, close enough for him to smell the sweet honey scent of her breath as it danced over his face. 'You just watch me, Rich Boy,' she said and then she swivelled on her trainer-clad feet and left.

CHAPTER TWO

'IT SAYS here that Andreas Ferrante and his mistress have broken up,' Kate Henley, Sienna's flatmate, said a couple of days later. She looked up over the newspaper and frowned. 'Hey, I thought you said they were about to get engaged?'

Sienna turned her back to wash a perfectly clean cup in the sink. 'What Andreas Ferrante does or doesn't do is of no interest to me whatsoever.'

'Hang on a minute…' The paper rustled as Kate spread it out over the clutter of the breakfast table. 'Oh, my God! Is it true?'

Sienna turned to see her flatmate's eyes were as big as the saucer she had just put on the draining rack. 'Is what true?' she asked warily.

'It says you're the other woman,' Kate said, gaping at her like a fish. 'It says *you're* the reason they broke up.'

'Let me see that.' Sienna frowned as she snatched up the paper. She scanned the article, her heart galloping like a spooked thoroughbred.

Mega-rich French-Italian furniture designer Andreas Ferrante admits his secret involvement with former housekeeper's daughter Sienna Baker destroyed his relationship with heiress Portia Briscoe.

'That's a downright lie!' Sienna slammed the paper down, knocking over the milk carton in the process. *'Oh, shoot!'* She grabbed a tea towel and mopped ineffectually at the mess while her mind ran on with fury.

'Why would he say something like that?' Kate asked with a wrinkled brow.

Sienna ground her teeth as she rinsed the cloth at the sink, splashing water everywhere in the process. 'He wants me to marry him, that's why.'

'Erm…did I hear you correctly?' Kate asked. 'I *think* you said he wants to marry you. Did you actually *say* that?'

Sienna flung the milk-sodden tea towel in the sink. 'I did but I'm not marrying him,' she said with a scowl.

Kate clutched a hand to her chest theatrically. 'Be still my heart,' she said. 'Andreas Ferrante—Florence-based millionaire, no, make that *billionaire* playboy—the most gorgeous-looking man on this planet—if not the entire universe—wants you to marry him and you said *no*?'

Sienna gave Kate an irritated look as she reached past her to wipe the milk off the bottom of the peanut butter jar. 'He's not that handsome.'

'Not handsome?' Kate gaped at her. 'What about his bank account?'

'I'm not interested in his bank account,' Sienna said. 'I married once for money. I'm not doing it again.'

'But I thought you really loved Brian Littlemore,' Kate said. 'You cried buckets at his funeral.'

Sienna thought of her late husband and how close she had become to him in the few months before he died. She had married him for protection and security, not love. It had been a knee-jerk reaction when her life had spun out of control soon after the death of her mother. After a horrifying incident in which she found herself in bed with a complete stranger after one too many drinks, Brian Littlemore had offered her security and respectability at a time in her life when she had neither. Like her, he had been forced to live a lie for most of his life, but during their marriage he had been honest with her in a way few people ever were. She had come to love him for it. As far as she was concerned, his secret had died with him. She would never betray his trust in her. 'Brian was a good man,' she said. 'He put his family before himself right to the day he died.'

'It's a pity he didn't leave you better provided for,' Kate said, reaching for the dishcloth. 'I guess you could always ask your rich twin sister to help you out with the rent if you don't manage to get a job in the next week or two.'

It still felt a little strange to Sienna to think of having a sister, let alone an identical twin. Gisele and she had been separated at birth when Sienna's mother had accepted a payout from the high profile Australian married man who had got her pregnant. Nell had taken Sienna and handed over Gisele to the childless couple, Hilary and Richard Carter, who had subsequently raised Gisele as their own. Nell had taken the secret to her grave. Sienna had found out quite by accident about Gisele's existence when she had been travelling in Australia a couple of months ago. She had only taken the trip on a whim when she'd seen a budget air fare online. She had always longed to go to Australia and, after Brian's death, it seemed a good opportunity to help her clear her head a bit before she made a decision about her future. A chance encounter in a department store had brought about her reunion with her twin.

Although Sienna loved Gisele dearly, she was still finding her feet with the relationship. Gisele had suffered a very bitter and painful breakup because of the sex tape scandal Sienna had been caught up in. Finding herself in that man's bed with no real memory of how she had got there had been such a shameful experience she had immediately left the country, thus having no idea of the fallout it had created for her sister. How that damning footage had got on the Internet and been wrongly linked to Gisele was something Sienna knew she would always feel dreadful about.

Gisele's fiancé Emilio had believed Gisele had betrayed him, and it had only been the discovery of the truth about Sienna's existence that had finally set things right. Their upcoming marriage in Rome was something she was looking forward to with bittersweet feelings. Her behaviour had almost wrecked Gisele and Emilio's lives. They had lost two precious years together and a baby. What could she ever do to make it up to them?

But Kate had made a very good point. She had to find a source of income and find it soon. Before he had become ill, Sienna had worked in the office of Brian's antiques business, but the family had stepped in after he had died and promptly sacked her. The trust fund Brian had left her had been just about gobbled up by the ongoing instability of the economy. Her dream of purchasing a home of her own had slipped out of her grasp, and there was no way—short of a miracle—for her to get it back.

Or was there?

Sienna thought of the money Guido Ferrante had bequeathed her. It was more than enough to buy a decent piece of real estate. The rest of it, invested sensibly, would set her up for life. She would be able to pursue her hobby of photography, perhaps even take it a step further and make a proper career out of it. How wonderful to be known for her talent instead of her mistakes and social blunders. How wonderful to be on the other side of the lens for a change, to be the one taking the pictures instead of being the subject.

She chewed at her lip as she thought of the conditions put on the will. Six months married to her worst enemy. It was a high price to pay, but then the reward at the end surely compensated for it?

It wasn't as if it had to be a *real* marriage.

An involuntary shiver rippled over her skin at the thought of lying in Andreas's strongly muscled arms, with his long hair-roughened legs entangled with hers, with his…

Sienna dried her hands on a fresh tea towel before she picked up her bag and keys. 'I'm going away,' she said. 'I'm not sure when I'll be back. I'll send you the money for the rent.'

Kate swung around with the empty milk carton in one hand and a wet dishcloth in the other. 'Away where?'

'To Florence.'

Kate's eyes bulged. 'You're going to say yes?'

Sienna gave her a grim look. 'This could turn out to be the longest six months of my life.'

'Six months?' Kate frowned in confusion. 'Isn't marriage meant to be until death us do part?'

'Not this one,' Sienna said.

'Aren't you going to pack?' Kate asked, eyes still out on stalks. 'You can't just turn up dressed in torn jeans and a T-shirt. You'll need clothes, lots and lots of clothes and shoes and make-up and stuff.'

Sienna flung her handbag strap over her shoulder. 'If Andreas Ferrante wants me to dress like one of his mistresses he can damn well pay for it. Ciao.'

'Signor Ferrante is in a design team meeting and cannot be disturbed,' the receptionist informed Sienna.

'Tell him his fiancée is here,' Sienna said with a guileless smile.

The receptionist's eyes widened as they took in Sienna's travel-worn appearance. 'I'm not sure…' she began uncertainly.

'Tell him if he doesn't see me right now the wedding won't go ahead,' Sienna said with a don't-mess-with-me look.

The receptionist reached for the intercom and spoke in Italian to Andreas. 'There's a young woman here who claims to be your fiancée. Do you want me to call Security?'

Andreas's deep mellifluous voice sounded over the system. 'Tell her to wait in Reception.'

Sienna leaned over the desk and swung the speaker her way. 'Get your butt out here, Andreas. We have things to discuss.'

'The boardroom,' he said. 'Ten minutes.'

'Out here *now*,' Sienna said through gritted teeth.

'*Cara,*' he drawled, 'such impatience fires my blood. Have you missed me terribly?'

Sienna pasted a false smile on her face for the sake of the receptionist. 'Darling, you can't imagine how *awful* it's been without your arms around me. I'm going crazy for you. It's been absolute torture to be without your kisses, your touch and your body doing all those wonderful things to—'

'Let's keep some things private, shall we?' he interjected coolly.

Sienna smiled at the now goggle-eyed receptionist. 'You wouldn't know it to look at him, but he has the most amazingly huge—'

'Sienna,' Andreas clipped out, 'get in here right *now*.'

Sienna slipped off the desk and gave the receptionist a fingertip wave. 'Isn't he adorable?'

The boardroom was empty by the time Sienna arrived. Andreas had a face like thunder and the air was crackling with palpable tension.

'What the hell do you think you're doing?' he asked even before she had closed the door.

Sienna threw him a contemptuous glare. 'Apparently we're engaged,' she said, clicking the door shut with considerable force. 'I read about it in the press.'

His mouth went to a flat line. 'I'm not the one who leaked that to the media.' He raked a hand through his hair. 'You know what they say about a woman scorned.'

Sienna raised her brows. 'Perfect Portia did that? Wow, I bet she didn't read that in the Good Girl's Guide to Avoiding Social Slip-Ups.'

His brows snapped together. 'I was about to ask her to marry me,' he said. 'She has a right to be upset.'

'My heart bleeds,' Sienna said on an exaggerated sigh.

He threw her a flinty look. 'Bitch.'

She smiled at him sweetly. 'Bastard.'

The air crackled some more.

Andreas paced the floor, his hand tracking another ragged pathway through the thick pelt of his hair. 'We have to find a way to manage this,' he said. 'Six months and we'll be free of this. I've looked at it from every angle. There's no way out of it. We just have to do what's expected. We can both win.'

Sienna pulled out one of the ergonomic chairs and sat down, swinging it from side to side as she watched him work the floor. 'What's in it for me?' she asked.

He stopped pacing to look at her, his frown deepening. 'What do you mean what's in it for you? You get a truckload of money at the end of it.'

She held his hazel gaze. 'I want more.'

His mouth tightened even further. 'How much more?'

'How about double?'

His jaw worked for a moment. 'A quarter.'

'A third,' she said, holding his look.

He slammed his hands on the table right in front of her, his face so close to hers she could smell the good quality coffee on his breath. 'Damn you to hell and back, you're not getting any more,' he said. 'The deal stands as it stands. I'm not negotiating on it.'

Sienna rolled her chair back and rose to her feet in one fluid movement. 'I guess that's it then,' she said. 'If you want me to marry you then you'll have to pay for the privilege.'

She was at the door when he finally spoke. 'All right,' he said on a heavily expelled breath. 'I'll give you a third on top of what my father bequeathed to you.'

Sienna turned to face him. 'You want that chateau real bad, don't you?'

His expression was rigid with tension. 'It belonged to my mother,' he said. 'I will do anything it takes to keep it out of the hands of my greedy, profligate second cousin.'

'Even marry me?'

He gave a humourless chuckle. 'I can't believe I'm saying this, but yes, I can actually think of worse things than marrying you.'

'Your imagination is streets ahead of mine because I *can't* think of anything worse than being married to you,' she said as she resumed her seat.

The air tightened like a steel cable.

Sienna felt his gaze run over her. It felt like a hot caress on her skin. His eyes seemed to sear the flesh off her bones. She felt naked under his scrutiny.

But then he *had* seen her naked, or almost.

She cringed at the memory. She had wanted him to be her first lover. She had dreamt about it for months. She had fantasised about him rescuing her from the life of drudgery she and her mother had been forced to live. All those years of never knowing what house they would be living in next. Not knowing what school or suburb she would be residing in. Her childhood had been a patchwork of packing up and leaving, of trying to fit in a new place, of trying to make friends with people who already had enough friends. She had always felt the odd one out. She didn't belong upstairs or downstairs.

But everything had changed when her mother had got the position as housekeeper at the Ferrante villa in Rome. It was the most stunning property, with fabulous gardens and a massive swimming pool and tennis court. It had felt like paradise after years of living in a variety of cramped and mouldy inner city flats.

It had been the first time in her life Sienna had seen her mother truly happy and settled. She hadn't wanted it to end. In her immature mind she'd had it all planned. Andreas, the son and heir of the Ferrante fortune, would fall in love with her and marry her. He was the handsome playboy prince, she was the pretty but penniless pauper, but their love and desire for each other would overcome that. She had been determined that he would notice her for once instead of treating her like an annoying puppy that hadn't been properly housetrained. To him, she had always been the cleaning lady's brat. He had even called her *enfant terrible*.

But this night it would be different. He hadn't been home in months. This time he would see the change in her. He would see her for the sexually mature young woman she had believed herself to be.

She had seen his hazel eyes follow her all evening when she had helped bring in the family's meal. She had sensed his male appraisal as she brought in the coffee and liqueurs to the *salone*. His nostrils had flared when she had leant down to place his cup beside him, as if he was breathing in her fragrance. Her hair had brushed against his arm and she had felt the electric current of awareness shoot through her body. He had looked at her then with those green and brown-flecked eyes of his and she had known he wanted her.

She had *felt* it.

She had waited for him in his bedroom, draping herself alluringly across his bed, dressed only in her knickers and bra, nervous but excited at the same time. Her body had tingled all over in anticipation.

The door had opened and Andreas had stood there for a moment, his eyes drinking in the sight of her. But then he seemed to give himself a mental shake and his expression immediately locked down, becoming stony, marble-like. 'What the hell do you think you're playing at?' he growled. 'Get dressed and get out.'

Sienna had been crushed. She had been so

certain he wanted her. She had seen it. She had felt it. She had sensed it in the air. The heavily charged atmosphere had practically exploded with erotic tension. The same tension she could see in his body even though he had done his best to hide it. 'I want you to make love to me,' she said. 'I know you want me. I've known it for ages.'

His mouth had been so tight it looked as if it had been drawn there with a thin felt tip pen. 'You're mistaken, Sienna,' he said. 'I have no interest in you whatsoever.'

Sienna had got off the bed and approached him. It had been brazen of her and impulsive but she had wanted to prove to him that what she felt was not just a figment of her youthful imagination. 'I want you, Andreas,' she said in a sultry tone as she reached for him.

Andreas had grasped her by the upper arms just as the door opened…

Sienna blinked herself out of the past. She didn't want to remember that dreadful scene between Andreas and his father. She didn't want to remember the unforgivable lies she had told. She had been desperate, terrified that her mother would lose the job she loved so much. The words had come tumbling out, a river of nonsense that she had regretted ever since. Andreas had never come home again, not even when his mother lay dying.

When Sienna looked up Andreas was standing behind the boardroom table, his steely gaze focused on her. 'There are some practicalities we need to sort out,' he said.

She resisted the urge to moisten her bark-dry lips. 'Practicalities?'

'The will states we have to live together as man and wife,' he said. 'That means you will have to sleep wherever I sleep.'

Sienna shot to her feet so fast the chair toppled over behind her. 'I'm not sleeping with you!'

He rolled his eyes as if dealing with an imbecile. 'Not in the same bed, Sienna, but under the same roof,' he said. 'We have to put on a show for the public.'

She blinked at him. 'You mean we have to act as if we really wanted to be married to each other?'

He continued to look at her with that un-wavering hazel gaze. 'As much as it pains me to say this, yes, we will have to act as if we're in love.'

'Are you out of your mind?' she gasped. 'I can't do that! Everyone knows how much I hate you.'

'Likewise,' he said dryly, 'but it's only for six months and it's only when we're in public. We can wrestle each other to the ground when we're alone.'

Sienna felt her cheeks flame with colour as the images his words conjured up flooded her brain. 'I haven't the faintest clue how to wrestle.'

'Perhaps I could teach you,' he said with a slanting smile that contained a hint of mockery and something else she didn't even want to think about identifying. 'The only thing you have to remember is the winner is the one who finishes on top.'

Sienna turned away so he couldn't see how hot and bothered she felt. Her body felt as if it were on fire. Her skin was prickling all over as she thought of his strong lean body pinning hers beneath his. 'How soon do we have to… you know…make things official?'

'As soon as possible,' he said. 'I've applied for a special licence. It should come through any day now.'

'And what sort of wedding do you have in mind?' she asked, turning to look at him again.

'You're surely not hankering for a white

wedding?' he said with a mocking arch of one of his eyebrows.

She gave him a flippant look in return. 'It's supposed to be the bride's day.'

'You've already been a bride.' He held her gaze for a microsecond before adding in disgust, 'To a man old enough to be your grandfather.'

Sienna raised her chin at him. 'At least I loved him.'

His lip curled. 'You loved his money, you trashy little gold-digger,' he said. 'Did he make you earn every penny by opening your legs on command?'

She gave him her wild-child smile, the one the press had documented time and time again—the one that painted her as a sleep-around-slut on the make. 'Wouldn't you like to know?' she asked.

He flung himself away from the table, thrusting his hands deep in his trouser pockets as if he didn't trust himself not to shake her till her teeth rattled.

Sienna found it exhilarating to know she had yanked his chain. He was always so cool and in control, but there was a side to him only she brought out. It was his primitive side, the raw male side that wanted to dominate and subdue her. The thought of him making her submit to him made her skin lift in a shiver.

She would fight him tooth and nail.

Andreas took some steadying breaths. She was doing it deliberately, of course. Trying her best to get under his skin, to prove nothing had changed in spite of the passage of time. How could one woman have such an effect on him?

He was *not* a slave to lust.

He had abhorred that in his father, how he had betrayed his wife of more than thirty years to bed a common tart.

Andreas prided himself on his self-control. He had the normal urges of any full-blooded male, but he always chose his partners with discretion. The women he slept with had class and poise. They were not headstrong harpies. They did not stir in him such unbridled passion.

He *never* lost his head.

But something about Sienna inflamed him and he had no control over it. He wanted to drive himself in her as hard and deeply as he could. He wanted to rut her like a wild animal did a random mate. He wanted to tame her, to have her submit to him in every way possible. His body ached and burned for her feverishly.

She was the forbidden fruit he had always prided himself he *could* resist.

That was no doubt why his father had set things up the way he had. He had known the temptation Sienna had always been for him. His father could not have thought of a worse punishment than tying her to him, dangling her under his nose, day in and day out. What had he been thinking? Had his father really hated him that much?

Andreas turned back to face Sienna. She was sitting down again, her jeans-clad legs propped up on the desk, her arms folded across her chest, which pushed her beautiful breasts upwards, looking every bit the impudent schoolgirl called into the headmaster's office. She had a lamentable disrespect for authority. She was wilful and defiant. She didn't know the meaning of the word respect. She could be surly and then sunny in the blink of an eye. She could be a sultry siren one second and an innocent waif the next.

He didn't have a clue how he was going to manage this farcical arrangement, but manage it he would, even if it meant sleeping with her to get her out of his system once and for all.

Every drop of his blood sizzled at the thought.

'Where are you staying?' he asked.

'I haven't found a place yet,' she said. 'I only just flew in.'

'Where are your things?'

'I didn't bring anything with me,' she said. 'I thought I'd leave the wardrobe arrangements up to you. I figured the stuff I normally wear won't suit.'

He stared at her incredulously. 'You came here with nothing but the clothes you're wearing?'

She gave him a feisty look. 'If I'm going to act the part, I need to dress for it. But you can pay for it, not me.'

'I have no problem with footing the bill,' Andreas said. 'It just seems a little unconventional, if not impetuous, for a young woman of your age to fly about the globe with nothing but jeans and a T-shirt and a handbag. Most of the women I know carry enough make-up and toiletries to sink a ship.'

'I'm very low maintenance,' she said.

'I very much doubt it,' he muttered.

She lowered her slim legs to the floor with a movement that was both coltish and graceful. 'I'll need a place to stay until we make things official,' she said. 'A five-star hotel will do nicely.'

'You can stay at my villa.' He scribbled the address on a sheet of paper and pushed it across the desk to her. 'I want you right under my nose where I can keep an eye on you.'

'You think I'll spill my guts to the press like your ex-fiancée did?' she asked with an insolent smile as she popped the folded paper inside her bra.

'Technically, she wasn't my fiancée,' he said, tearing his gaze away from the tempting sight of her pert breasts. 'I hadn't got that far. I had bought a ring, however. You can borrow it if you like.'

She gave him a slitted-eye glare. 'Don't even think about it, Rich Boy,' she said. 'I want my own ring, not someone else's.'

Andreas came over to where she was standing. He could feel the force field of her as soon as he crossed that invisible line. Her summery fragrance assaulted his nostrils, a combination of flowers and feminine warmth that was as heady as any mind-altering drug. This close, he could see the tiny dusting of freckles over the bridge of her retroussé nose and the tiniest of chickenpox scars above her left eyebrow.

Almost of its own volition, his gaze flicked down to her mouth.

Lust gave him a knockout punch in the gut

when he saw the way the tip of her tongue darted out to leave a glistening layer of moisture on those plump, ripe lips.

He fought his leaping pulse back under control, dragging his gaze back to her glittering one. 'This is all a game to you, isn't it?' he said.

Her top lip curled at him and her grey-blue eyes glittered. 'You were going to kiss me, weren't you?'

Andreas ground his teeth until he thought he'd have to eat jelly for the rest of his life. 'I want to throttle you, not kiss you,' he said.

'You put one finger on me and see what happens,' she said, matching him stare for stare.

Andreas already knew what would happen. He could feel it in his body. It was thundering through his veins like a torpedo. He couldn't think of a time when he had felt such forceful, uncontrollable desire. It was like being a hormone-driven teenager all over again. Dynamite couldn't do more damage than Sienna in temptress mode. 'Get out of my sight,' he ground out savagely.

She put up her chin. 'Say please.'

He strode over to the door, holding it open pointedly. 'Out.'

She tossed the silver-blonde curtain of her

hair back behind her shoulders. 'If I'm going to stay at your place I'll need a key,' she said.

'The housekeeper will let you in,' Andreas said. 'I'll call her now and tell her to expect you.'

'What will you tell her and the rest of your staff about us?' she asked.

'I don't make a habit of exchanging confidences with the household staff at any of my residences,' he said. 'They will assume it's a normal marriage, just like everyone else.'

A little frown appeared over her grey-blue eyes. 'Even though we won't be sharing a room?'

Andreas felt that punch to his gut again. He could think of nothing more tempting than rolling around his bed with her legs wrapped around his waist, his body buried to the hilt in hers. His blood thickened and pulsed as he thought of how it would feel to finally satiate this need he had harboured so long. He would have his fill of her once and for all. In six months he would walk away. He would finally be immune. Free. In control.

'It's very common for people with villas the size of mine to occupy different suites,' he said. 'It doesn't make sense to cram into one room when there are thirty others to choose from.'

Her eyes went wide. 'That big, huh?'

'It's bigger than my father's.'

A little smile played about the corners of her mouth. 'I just bet it is,' she said.

Andreas took out his wallet and handed her a credit card. 'Here,' he said, handing it to her. 'Go shopping. Get your hair and nails done. Have coffee. Have a meal. I won't be back till late. Don't wait up.'

She took the card from him without touching his fingers and popped it in her bag. She moved past him in the doorway, not touching but close enough for every hair on his body to stand to attention and for every blood vessel to expand and throb. He was about to let out the breath he was holding when she suddenly stopped and turned back to look at him. 'Do you have any idea why your father did this?' she asked.

'No idea at all.'

She chewed at her lower lip for a moment, a shadow passing like a cloud over her face. 'He must have really hated me…'

'What makes you think that?' he asked, frowning at her. 'This is about me, not you. My father hated me as much as I hated him.'

A little beat of silence passed.

'I'd better get going,' she said with an overly

bright smile. 'So many things to buy, so little time. Ciao.'

Andreas closed the door once she had left and leant back against it heavily, a frown tugging at his forehead. Half an hour with Sienna was like being in the middle of a hurricane with nothing but a paper parasol for protection.

How was he going to get through six months?

CHAPTER THREE

SIENNA took a taxi to Andreas's Tuscan estate once she had finished shopping. The Renaissance-style villa was a few kilometres outside Florence, set amongst acres of olive groves and vineyards in the Chianti region of Tuscany, made famous for its wine. The fading afternoon sunshine cast a spectacular light over the fresh growth on the vines. Flowers in an array of bright colours tumbled from baskets hanging near the entrance to the villa. It was breathtakingly beautiful and a jolting reminder of the wealth Andreas had been born into and had never questioned. Sure, he had forged his own way with his furniture designs, but he had never had to worry about bills not being paid or where the next meal was coming from. It was hard not to feel a teensy bit jealous. Why did he even want his mother's wretched chateau in Provence when he had all of this?

The thought of owning a property like the chateau made Sienna wonder if she should set about making him default on the will by making it impossible to live with her. It was a tempting thought: a chateau of her own, her own patch of paradise. It wasn't as if Andreas would be left homeless or anything. He had homes everywhere. The one in Florence was his base, but she knew for a fact he had a villa in Barbados as well as one somewhere in Spain.

The door of the villa opened and a motherly-looking woman who introduced herself as Elena smiled as she ushered Sienna in. 'Signor Ferrante told me you would be arriving this evening,' she said. 'I have made up the Rose Suite for you.' She winked knowingly. 'It is right next to his.'

Sienna forced a smile. 'That was very thoughtful of you.'

'It is no trouble,' Elena said. 'I was young and madly in love once. I met my husband and within a month we were married. I knew Signor Ferrante would change his mind about that one.'

Sienna frowned slightly. 'Erm…"That one"?'

Elena made a noise that sounded something like a snort. 'Princess Portia. She was never happy. I had to fetch and carry. She did not like red meat. She did not like cheese. She only ate this. She only ate that. I nearly went crazy.'

'Maybe she was thinking of her figure,' Sienna offered generously.

The housekeeper gave another snort of disapproval. 'She is not the right one for Signor Ferrante,' she said. 'He needs a woman who is as passionate as he is.'

Sienna couldn't help wondering exactly what Andreas had told his housekeeper about their relationship or whether Elena had assumed their whirlwind courtship had come about because they had suddenly fallen deeply in love. Or, even more worryingly, could the housekeeper see something in Sienna that she desperately wanted to keep hidden? It wasn't as if she still had a crush on Andreas or anything. She didn't love him. She hated him. But that didn't mean his physical presence didn't disturb her. It did, and way too much. 'You seem to know him very well,' she said.

Elena smiled. 'He's a good man. He's very generous and hard-working, too. He helps in the vineyard whenever he can, and the orchards. You knew him before? I read about it in the paper. Your *mamma* used to work for his family, *sì*?'

'*Sì,*' Sienna said. 'My mother took up the position as head housekeeper when I was fourteen. Andreas wasn't living at home then, of course, but we ran into each other from time to time.'

'Friends to lovers, *sì*?' Elena said, smiling broadly.

'Erm…something like that.'

'I can see the fire in your eyes,' Elena said. 'He will be happy with you. I can tell these things. You will make good babies with him, *sì*?'

Sienna felt her face grow hot. 'We haven't talked about kids. It's been a bit of a whirlwind affair, actually.'

'The best ones are,' Elena said with matronly authority. 'Come, I'll show you your new home. You'll want to settle in before Signor Ferrante gets back.'

Sienna followed the cheery housekeeper on a tour of the villa. It was even bigger than she had expected. Room after room, suite after suite, all beautifully and tastefully decorated. It occurred to her that in a villa this size she could pass six months without even running into Andreas, or anyone else for that matter.

'I'll leave you to shower and change,' Elena said. 'I will set up the dinner before I leave.'

'You don't live here?' Sienna asked.

'I live in the farmhouse next to the olive grove,' Elena said. 'My husband, Franco, works for Signor Ferrante too. If you want anything we are only a phone call away. I will be back in the morning around ten. Signor Ferrante likes a bit of privacy. He has lived with servants all his life. I understand he wants his space.'

Sienna hadn't factored in actually being alone with Andreas. Alone with servants was a whole lot different than *alone*. It put a completely different spin on things. Could she trust him to keep his distance? The chemistry between them was volatile, to say the least. She knew it wouldn't take much to set things off. If that tense little moment in his boardroom was anything to go by, things could get pretty intense in a flash and what would she be able to do about it? It wasn't as if she had any immunity, not really. She put on a good front but how long was that going to last? He had only to look at her a certain way and her insides coiled with lust.

It was ironic because sex was something she had never really taken to with any great enthusiasm. Although she had partied, and partied hard after Andreas's rejection, it had been months and months before she had even thought about dating, and even when she had finally gone out with a couple of young men her age, the intimate encounters had left her cold. She had felt nothing for either of her partners and they clearly had felt nothing for her. And then, after the shameful night that had found her in a stranger's bed, she had locked herself away in a sex-less and safe marriage of convenience. Before that night, whenever the press had portrayed her as a sleep-around-slut, she had laughed it off, pleased that she was getting some attention, even if it wasn't positive. *She* had known the truth about herself and that had been all that mattered. But now the label had a ring of truth to it she dearly wished she could remove.

After she had unpacked and showered and changed, Sienna came downstairs. The villa seemed rather empty without the warm and friendly chatter of the housekeeper. She picked at some food and poured herself a glass of wine, feeling restless and irritable.

Maybe she should have thought about this a little more before she went any further. It wasn't the first time her impulsive nature had got her into trouble. Was it too late to back out?

The money stopped her thoughts of escape

in their tracks. What was she thinking? It was like any other unpleasant job that had to be done. A six-month contract that would be over before she knew it. She would receive a handsome pay-out for her trouble.

There was that T word again. Trouble.

She had a habit of attracting it, no matter what she did. Was she forever destined to be at the mercy of circumstances she couldn't control? Was it her fault her mother had kept her and given away her sister?

Jealousy was something Sienna didn't want to feel around her twin, but she couldn't help feeling a little cheated by how things had panned out. Gisele had grown up well provided for. She'd had a private education and gone on fabulous exotic holidays. She had lived in the same gorgeous house all of her childhood. She hadn't had to pack up her things every few months or so when someone got tired of her mother's laziness or cheek. She'd had a father to watch out for her, to provide for her and protect her from those who preyed upon the vulnerable.

Sienna, on the other hand, had grown up a whole lot faster than her peers. She'd learnt early on that there were few people you could trust. Everyone was out for his or her own gain.

And now she was no different.

She would get what she could out of this and move on. She would milk Andreas for every penny she could before she walked out of his life.

For good.

Sienna was on to her second glass of wine when she heard Andreas's car. The deep throaty roar of the engine made her stomach clench unexpectedly. His fast car, fast-living lifestyle was something that had always attracted her even as it annoyed her. He had probably never had to push start a car in his life. He had never had to make his own bed or butter his own toast. He hadn't been born with just a silver spoon in his mouth, but an entire dinner service. He ate from fine bone china and drank from crystal glasses. He had everything that money could buy and then some.

How she hated him for it.

Andreas came in to find Sienna lying on her stomach on his leather sofa with a half drunk glass of wine in her hand and the remote control to his big screen television in the other. Her hair was pulled back in a high ponytail and she was wearing close-fitting black yoga pants and a loose hot-pink top that had slipped off one of her sun-kissed shoulders. Her feet were bare as she swung her lower legs back and forth in a slow motion kicking action. She looked young and nubile and so damned sexy he felt a tight ache deep in his groin.

'Hard day at the office?' she asked without even looking his way as she flicked through the channels.

He tugged at his tie to loosen it. 'You could say that.' He shrugged off his jacket and tossed it over the end of the other sofa. 'Making ourselves at home, are we?'

She took a sip of her wine before she answered. 'Having a blast,' she said. 'You make great wine, by the way. I like your house-keeper too. We're already best friends.'

'You're not supposed to make friends with the servants,' he said, frowning.

She muted the television and swung her legs down to sit up. 'Why's that?' she asked. 'Because they might forget their place and get too close to you?'

Andreas let out a carefully controlled breath. 'They're employees, not friends,' he said. 'They do the work and they get paid. There's nothing else that's required of them.'

She got off the sofa and padded over to

where he was standing with her loose-limbed sensual gait. She looked up at him with those big sparkling-with-mischief grey-blue eyes of hers and he felt his groin tighten another excruciating notch. It was all he could do to stand there without hauling her against him to show her how much he lusted after her. But he had decided he would have her when *he* said so, not because she thought she could manipulate him at will.

'Have you eaten?' she asked.

'What is this?' he asked with a mocking look. 'Wifely duties 101?'

She lifted that deliciously bare shoulder of hers in a little shrug, her mouth going to a resentful pout. 'Just trying to be helpful,' she said. 'I thought you looked tired.'

'Maybe that's because I haven't slept a wink since I heard about my father's will,' Andreas said, rubbing a hand over his face, which was in need of a shave.

He walked over to the bar and poured himself a glass of the wine Sienna had opened. He took a couple of sips before swinging his gaze back to her. 'I've got the licence. I pulled a few strings. We can get married next Friday.'

Her eyes widened a fraction but her voice

when she spoke was all sass. 'You move fast when you want something, don't you, Rich Boy?'

'No point in dragging things out,' he said. 'The sooner we marry, the sooner we can get a divorce.'

'Sounds like a plan.'

Andreas narrowed his gaze in sharp focus. 'What's that supposed to mean?'

Her slim brows lifted archly. 'Exactly what I said,' she said. 'You seem to have it all figured out.'

'I do,' he said. 'We marry and then at the end of six months we end it. Simple.'

'What did you tell Elena about us?' she asked.

'Nothing, other than we're getting married as soon as possible.'

'You must have said more than that,' she said, toying with the end of her ponytail.

'Why do you think that?' he asked.

She lifted her golden shoulder up and down again. 'She seems to think we're madly in love,' she said.

'Most people are when they marry,' Andreas said, taking another mouthful of wine.

A beat of silence ticked past.

'Were you in love with Portia Briscoe?' Sienna asked.

Andreas's brows shot together. 'What sort of question is that?' he asked.

She tilted her head on one side, her finger tapping against her lips. 'No, I don't think you loved her,' she said. 'I think you liked her well enough. She ticked all the boxes for you. She comes from money, she knows what cutlery to use and she dresses well and never has a hair out of place. She never says the wrong thing or rubs people up the wrong way. But grab-you-in-the-guts love? Nope. I don't think so.'

'You're a fine one to harp on about true love,' he said. 'You weren't in love with Brian Littlemore. You barely knew him when you waltzed him down the aisle before his wife was even cold in her grave.'

'Actually, I did know him,' she said with an imperious air. 'I'd met him well before his wife died.'

Andreas gave her a disgusted look. 'And no doubt you opened your legs for him then too. Did he pay you? Or did you give him one for free to get him so hot and hungry the poor old fool couldn't help himself?'

Sienna's eyes flashed at him with undiluted venom. 'You have a mind like a sewer,' she said. 'You sit up there in your diamond-encrusted, gold-inlaid ivory tower of yours,

passing judgement on people you don't even
know from a bar of soap. Brian was a decent
man with a big heart. You haven't even got
a heart. All you've got inside your chest is a
lump of cold, hard stone.'

Andreas took a measured sip of his wine.
'Your loyalty to your late husband is touching, *ma chérie*,' he said. 'But I wonder if you
would be so loyal if you knew he had another
lover the whole time he was with you.'

Her eyes flickered before moving away
from his. He watched as she moved back
to where she had left her glass of wine. She
picked it up and cradled it in her hands without drinking any of it. 'We had an open marriage,' she said, still not looking at him. 'It
gave us both the freedom to do what we
wanted as long as we were both discreet about
it.'

Andreas wondered if he should have been
quite so blunt with her. There had been nothing in the press about her late husband's affair. He had heard it second-hand and not
from a particularly reliable source. But if she
was hurt or upset by the news she was doing
a good job of concealing it. Admittedly, she
was standing stiffly, almost guardedly, but
neither her expression nor her tone showed
any sign of emotional carnage.

'You knew about his mistress?' he asked.

She turned to look at him, a little puzzled frown pulling at her brow. 'His...mistress?'

'The woman he was seeing,' he said. 'His lover.'

She gave a little laugh that seemed totally out of place. It sounded almost...relieved. 'Oh, *her*...' she said. 'Yes, I knew about her right from the start.'

'And you married Littlemore anyway?' he asked, frowning deeply.

She met his gaze with a directness he found jarring. 'I did it for the money,' she said. 'The same reason I'm marrying you. It's only for the money.'

Andreas felt his jaw clamp down in anger. She was so brazen about her gold-digging motives. Had she no shame? No self-respect? What sort of laughing stock would she try and make of him during their six-month marriage? She had no sense of propriety. She was as selfish and self-serving as she had been as a teenager. She would do anything to get as much out of this situation as she could. He could practically see the dollar signs flashing in her eyes. 'While we're on the subject of money,' he said, 'I want to make a few things clear, right from the start. Throughout the duration of our marriage, I will not tolerate any behaviour on your part that leads to speculation in the press that this is not a normal relationship. If you don't behave yourself there will be consequences. Do I make myself clear?'

She gave him one of her insolent schoolgirl looks. 'Perfectly.'

He drew in a breath for patience and slowly released it. 'Secondly, I will not be made a fool of by your practice of leaping in and out of bed with a host of unsavoury men,' he said. 'That means no boudoir photos and no seedy little sex tapes uploaded to the Internet or social networking sites. Got it?'

Her cheeks turned a cherry-red, he presumed from anger at being reminded of the sex tape incident that had occurred a little over two years ago, for which her twin sister had inadvertently taken the rap. He'd missed the scandal as he had been abroad at the time, but, after reading about her twin's recent reconciliation with her fiancé, the thing that had struck him most was that Sienna hadn't come forward at the time. To be fair, she hadn't known she even had a twin then, but it was just typical of Sienna's inability or unwillingness to take responsibility for her actions. She didn't give a toss what anyone else suffered because of her reprehensible behaviour.

She just barrelled her way through life with no thought or care for what anyone else was feeling.

'There won't be any slip-ups,' she said stiffly.

'There had better not be,' he warned.

She turned away from him and drained her glass, putting it down with a little rattle against the coffee table. 'Will that be all?' she asked.

Andreas pressed his lips together. Her subdued tone was a new one. He hadn't heard her use it before. How did she do it? How did she switch things so deftly to make him feel as if *he* had overstepped the mark? 'If it is any consolation to you, I will also refrain from any behaviour that could compromise our arrangement,' he said, ploughing a hand through his hair. 'It's only for six months. A bout of celibacy is supposed to re-energise the soul and sharpen the intellect, or so I've heard.'

She gave him a little smile, that old familiar spark back in her gaze. 'Do you think you'll last the distance?' she asked.

Andreas wasn't prepared to put any money on it. Not with her looking so damned hot and gorgeous without even trying. 'I'll take it one day at a time,' he said, deliberately running his gaze over her from head to toe and back again.

She held his look but he noticed one of her shoulders rolling as if she suddenly found her clothes prickly against her skin. 'Good luck with that,' she said in an airy tone.

He refilled his wine glass and took a couple of mouthfuls before he turned to look at her again. 'By the way, I'd appreciate you making an effort to buy something suitable to wear to the wedding. I'm not sure yoga pants or tattered jeans are going to set a new trend in bridal gear, no matter how good you look in them.'

Sienna raised her brows at him. 'My, oh, my, a compliment from the impossible-to-impress Signor Ferrante,' she said. 'Wonders will never cease.'

Andreas frowned at her in irritation. 'What are you talking about? I've complimented you plenty of times.'

'Remind me of one,' she said, folding her arms across her chest as she tilted one hip forwards in a pose of youthful scepticism. 'My memory seems to have completely failed me.'

He rubbed at the back of his neck. 'What about the time you were going to that school dance when you were sixteen or thereabouts,' he said. 'You were wearing a crinkly candy-pink and white dress. I said you looked pretty.'

She gave him a resentful look. 'You said I looked like a cupcake.'

Andreas felt a smile tug at his mouth. 'Did I really say that?'

'You did.'

'Well, then, what I probably meant to say was you looked good enough to eat,' he said.

The air seemed to thicken in the ensuing silence.

'You probably should take a little more care with your diet,' Sienna said. 'Too much sugar is bad for you.'

'Yes, but once in a while it's good to have a little of what you fancy, don't you think?' Andreas said.

'Only if you can keep control,' she said, holding his look with a haughty air he found incredibly arousing. 'For some people, one taste is never going to be enough. They can't just have one square of chocolate. They have to have the whole bar.'

His gaze swept over her slim figure again. 'You're obviously not speaking from personal experience,' he said. 'I could just about span your waist with my hands.'

'Lucky genes, I guess.'

Andreas saw a flicker of something move

through her gaze. 'What are you going to tell your sister about this arrangement between us?' he asked.

She rolled her lips together for a moment. 'I feel uncomfortable about lying to her, but I don't want her to worry about me either,' she said. 'I think it's best if I stick to the script for now.'

'We should probably tidy up a few details then,' Andreas said. 'Like how we came to fall in love so quickly.'

Sienna gave him one of her worldly looks. 'Do you really think people are going to believe you fell in love with me? We have nothing in common. I'm a cleaning lady's kid from the wrong side of the tracks. You've had more silver spoons in your mouth than most people have had hot dinners. Men with your sort of heritage don't marry trailer trash. It's just in fairy tales where that sort of thing happens. Not in real life.'

Andreas frowned. 'That's rather a harsh way to speak of your background,' he said. 'I have never once referred to you as trailer trash.'

'You don't have to,' she said. 'I see it in your eyes every time you look at me.'

He felt a little stab of guilt. He had called her plenty of other things in the past and none of them were any less disparaging. 'Look, Sienna,' he said. 'I realise we have some ill feeling because of our history. But I'm prepared to put that aside for the moment in order to get through this period.'

She chewed at her lower lip in a childlike manner he found at odds with what he knew of her. 'Are you saying you forgive me?' she asked.

'I wouldn't go as far as saying that,' he said. 'What you did was unforgivable.'

'Yes,' she said, biting down on her lip again. 'I know...'

Andreas ratcheted up his resolve. She was toying with him, trying to appeal to his better side to get herself off the hook. He wasn't buying it for a moment. Behind that forgive-me-I-was-too-young-to-know-what-I-was-doing façade was a conniving little social-climbing trollop who was on a mission to land herself a fortune. She might have fooled his father into writing her into the will, but it wasn't going to work on him.

He scooped up his jacket from the sofa. 'I'm going to be tied up for the next few days,' he said. 'I hope you can stay out of mischief until Friday.'

'It'll be a piece of cake,' she said.

He gave her a droll look before he left. 'Just stick to one slice, OK?'

CHAPTER FOUR

WHEN Sienna came down after a shower the next morning there was no sign of Andreas. Elena hadn't yet arrived so it gave her some time to wander about and get her bearings. She made a cup of tea and took it out onto a wisteria-covered terrace. She felt the heat of the sun-warmed flagstones through the bare soles of her feet as she walked towards one of the wrought iron chairs. She sat and looked out at the expansive view. There were a hundred shades of green and a thousand fragrant smells and sounds to dazzle her senses.

She put her cup down and went back inside to get her camera from her handbag. It was compact but high-tech enough to allow her to capture images that took her fancy. She went back down to the terrace and beyond, snapping away in bliss, losing track of time as she explored the gardens.

She was aiming for a shot of a bird on a

shrub when she caught sight of a dog skulking in the distance. She lowered the camera and, shading her eyes with one of her hands, peered to see if anyone was with it. It seemed to be alone and, by the look of its sunken-in sides, half starving.

Sienna looped her camera strap around her wrist and walked towards the dog. 'Here, boy,' she called when she got a little closer. 'Come here and say hello.'

The dog looked at her warily, the back of its neck going up in stiff bristles.

Sienna was undaunted. She crouched down and crooned to the dog softly, holding out her hand for it to smell. The dog crept closer, its body low to the ground, the hackles going down and its tail giving the tiniest of wags. 'Good boy,' she said. 'That's right; I won't hurt you. Good dog.'

Just as she was about to see if the dog's worn collar had an identifying tag on it, there was a sound behind her and the dog tore off, disappearing into the nearby woods with its tail tucked between its legs.

'You little fool,' Andreas said. 'You'll get yourself bitten. That dog is a stray. Franco was supposed to shoot it days ago.'

Sienna rose from her crouching position but, even so, he seemed to tower over her.

'But it's wearing a collar!' she said. 'It must belong to someone. Maybe it's just lost and can't find its way home.'

'It's a flea-bitten mongrel,' he said. 'Any fool can see that.'

Sienna scowled at him. 'I suppose you only allow pure-bred dogs with pedigree papers the thickness of three phone books on your precious property.' She brushed past him to go back to the villa. 'What a stuck-up jerk.'

He caught her arm on the way past, swinging her round to face him. 'You shouldn't be wandering around down here without shoes,' he said. 'Are you completely without sense?'

Sienna tugged at his hold but it tightened like a vice. She felt the sexy rasp of his callused fingers on her wrist and her stomach gave a little fluttery flip-flop. She met his hard hazel eyes and something shifted in the atmosphere. Her gaze slipped to his mouth. He hadn't yet shaved and the sexy pepper of his stubble sent another shockwave of awareness through her. He smelt of man and heat and hard work, a potent smell that stirred her feminine senses into a mad frenzy. Could he tell how much he got under her skin? Could he sense it? Was that why he kept looking at her with those smouldering eyes? 'What would you care?' she said. 'I'd be better off to you dead, wouldn't I?'

His brooding frown cut deeper into his tanned forehead. 'That's a crazy thing to say,' he said. 'Why would I want you dead?'

'Because you'd automatically inherit the chateau,' she said. 'You wouldn't have to go through a marriage you didn't want to a woman you hate more than anyone else in the world.'

'You hate me just as much as I hate you, so we're pretty square on that,' he said. 'Or are you hiding a secret affection for me, hmm?'

She gave him a withering look. 'You have got to be joking.'

He tugged her closer, flush against his rock-hard body. The heat of his arousal was like a brand against her belly. 'You like to tease and tantalise, don't you, *cara*?' he said. 'You like the power. It's like a drug to you, to have men falling over themselves to possess you. I see it in your eyes. They dance with sensual intent. You can't wait to have me fall at your feet. But I won't do it. I won't let you play your seductress games with me. I will have you on my terms, not yours.'

Sienna pushed against his chest with the flat of her hands but, while it put some distance between their upper bodies, it made their lower connection all the more intense. She felt the thundering roar of his blood against her, the rigid length of him taking her breath clean away.

The air sizzled with sexual electricity.

She felt the force of it like waves of searing heat rippling over her skin. She felt her heart rate pick up and her inner core clenched and released, clenched and released, in a primitive rhythm of need.

She wondered if he was going to kiss her. His eyes had dropped to her mouth in an infinitesimal moment of sensual suspense that made her heart beat all the faster. She sent her tongue out over her lips, wondering what he would taste like. Would he be rough or smooth? Forceful or gentle?

'Damn you,' Andreas ground out as he put her from him roughly. 'Damn you to hell.'

Sienna let out a ragged breath as she watched him stride back the way he had come. She put a hand to her chest where her heart was beating like a maniacal metronome. She felt light-headed and shaky on her feet, her body still tingling from the hard male contact of his. That primitive pulse of longing was still thrumming deep inside her and she couldn't seem to turn it off.

She looked down at her wrist where her

camera was swinging from its strap. The imprint of his fingers was almost visible on her skin. She touched the tender area with the fingertips of her other hand, her stomach slipping like a skater who had mistimed a manoeuvre.

She was in trouble with a capital T.

Sienna didn't see Andreas until the evening before the wedding. Elena told her he had been called away to some important business in Milan but Sienna wondered if he was keeping his distance for as long as possible before they were thrust together as man and wife.

The days flashed past as she fielded phone calls from Gisele and her flatmate Kate in London. Somehow she managed to convince her twin she was madly and blissfully in love with Andreas and couldn't wait to get married. As Gisele's wedding was in a few weeks' time and the guest list had blown out considerably, Gisele was nothing but supportive of Sienna's plan for a simple witnesses-only ceremony so she and Andreas could be left alone by the press.

Kate didn't buy into the 'we suddenly fell in love' story but, as a hopeless romantic herself, she was convinced Andreas would finally come to his senses and want Sienna to stay with him for ever.

Sienna didn't like to disabuse her friend of the impossibility of such an outcome. His refusal to forgive her was not the only stumbling block to their relationship. She had long ago given up her foolish dream of him falling in love with her. And, as for her falling in love with him, well, that was *not* going to happen.

Sienna went shopping a couple of times under the escort of a very willing Franco, who faithfully carried her bags and waited patiently in the car while she had her hair and beauty treatments done.

There was also a visit to a lawyer's office where Andreas had set up the signing of a prenuptial agreement. Sienna understood it was part and parcel of many modern marriages, and she totally understood Andreas's motivations given the wealth he had at his disposal, but even so it rankled that he didn't trust her to walk away without a legal tussle when the time was up on their marriage.

The rest of the time Sienna spent working on befriending the dog, whom she called Scraps. He had built up enough confidence to take titbits of food from her hand, but he wouldn't allow her to touch him as yet. She was prepared to be patient, however. And she had made Franco promise he wouldn't shoot him, no matter what orders Andreas gave to the contrary.

Sienna had not long fed the dog and settled him in one of the buildings close to the villa when she heard the roar of Andreas's car come up the driveway that curved through the property, fields of vines on one side, olive groves on the other. A church bell calling the faithful to Mass sounded in the distance, a peaceful sound that was totally at odds with the tension she could feel building in her body as soon as Andreas came into view.

She watched as he unfolded his long, lean length from the low-slung vehicle. He had loosened his tie and his shirtsleeves were rolled up past his strongly muscled wrists. His suit jacket was hooked through one of his fingers and was slung over his shoulder, his briefcase in his other hand.

His eyes ran over her shorts and T-shirt, resting a heart-stopping moment on the upthrust of her breasts, before meshing with her gaze. 'Isn't it supposed to be bad luck to see the bride before the wedding?' he asked.

'That's the morning of the wedding,' she said. 'I don't think the night before counts.'

He gave a slight movement of his lips that could only be very loosely described as a smile, and a half one at that. 'Glad to hear it,' he said. His footsteps crunched over the gravel as he came to where she was standing. 'Elena tells me you have a new conquest.'

'That would be Scraps,' Sienna said, rocking on her feet. 'I've just tucked him in for the night.'

One brow curved in an arch over his eye. 'Scraps?' he said.

'It's what he likes to eat,' she said. 'Plus it's sort of a tribute to his mixed heritage.'

His mouth quirked upwards in that almost smile again. 'Original.'

'I thought so.'

He indicated for her to go ahead of him into the villa. 'How has your week been?' he asked.

'I've shopped myself silly,' Sienna said. 'Thanks for the use of the car, by the way. Franco quite fancies himself as a chauffeur. I think you should get him fitted for a uniform.'

Andreas closed the door and placed his car keys on a marble table in the foyer. 'I've ordered a car for you,' he said. 'It should be here some time next week.'

'I hope it's an Italian sports car,' Sienna said, just to needle him. 'I'll be the envy of all my friends. It's the ultimate status symbol.'

He gave her a derisive look. 'It will get you

from A to B without mishap, that is if you drive with any sense of responsibility. But, judging by what you do in your personal life, I'm not holding my breath.'

'I'll have you know I'm a very safe driver,' Sienna said, following him into the *salone*. 'I've never had an accident or even copped a speeding fine. Parking tickets, well, now, that's another thing.'

'So you have a history of outstaying your welcome, do you?' he asked as he poured himself a drink. 'I'll have to make a note of that.'

Sienna threw him a haughty look. 'If you think I'll stay even a minute over the six months, then you are seriously deluded,' she said.

He looked at her with his unwavering hazel gaze. It seemed more brown than green in the subdued lighting of the *salone*. But then she had noticed lately that his eyes seemed to change with his mood. 'Just as long as we're both clear on the terms of this arrangement,' he said. 'I don't want any complications. And you, *cara,* are nothing if not a magnet for complications.'

Only Andreas could make a term of endearment sound like an insult, Sienna thought. But she had to concede that he was right about the complications. Other people had such simple, uncomplicated lives. She seemed to go from one stuff-up to another. It was as if she had been cursed since birth. But then, maybe she had. Born out of wedlock to a man who had used her mother and then tossed her aside when he was done with her, taking one of her babies for a sum of money to pay for her silence.

It didn't get more complicated or cursed than that.

Sienna suddenly realised Andreas was still watching her with that slightly narrowed focused gaze of his. 'Are you going to offer me a drink or should I just help myself?' she asked.

'Pardon my oversight,' he said. 'What would you like?'

'White wine,' she said. 'The one from your vineyard. It's my favourite.'

He handed her a chilled glass of wine but, just as she reached for it, his brows moved together as he saw the fading marks on her arm. 'What happened to your wrist?' he asked.

Sienna put her hand back down by her side. 'Nothing.'

He put the wine aside and reached for her hand, gently turning over her wrist to look at the full set of his fingerprints there. She saw his face flinch with shock. 'Did I do this to you?' he asked.

'It's nothing,' she said. 'I bruise easily, that's all.'

Her stomach folded over as the pad of his thumb gently moved across the purple stain of his touch. 'Forgive me,' he said in a voice so deep it felt as if it had come from beneath the floor at their feet.

She swallowed as his eyes meshed with hers. 'Really, Andreas, it's nothing...'

'Does it hurt?' he asked, still gently cradling her wrist in the warmth of his hand.

Sienna wasn't used to this tender, more considerate side of him. It made something inside her melt like molasses under the blaze of a hot summer sun. A dangerous melting that she should not allow, but somehow she couldn't prevent it. It flowed through her like a slow-moving tide, all the way through the circuitry of her veins, loosening her spine and all of her ligaments until she felt as if she would end up in a pool of longing at his feet. Her swiftly indrawn breath hitched against something in her throat. 'No...'

He brought her wrist up to his mouth, his lips barely touching the sensitive skin, but it set off a shower of sensations that travelled all the way up her arm and shoulder, making every hair on her head lift away from her scalp.

His eyes were the darkest she had ever seen them. 'It won't happen again,' he said. 'I can assure you of that. You have no reason to fear for your safety while living under my protection.'

'Thanks for the reassurance,' Sienna said, pulling her hand out of his with a sassy little smile to hide her vulnerability, 'but I've never been scared of you.'

'No, you haven't, have you?' he said, still studying her intently.

Sienna picked up the wine he had poured for her earlier. 'So, I take it we're not going on a honeymoon?' she said before taking a sip.

'On the contrary,' he said, 'I thought we should go to Provence. It's a perfect opportunity to pretend we are taking some time together. I want to see how the Chateau de Chalvy estate is being run. My father appointed a husband and wife team to manage it quite a few years back. I'd like to reacquaint myself with them.'

'Why don't you go on your own?' Sienna said. 'It's not as if you really need me to tag along. I'll only get in the way or say something I shouldn't or dress inappropriately.'

'Sienna, we are getting married tomorrow,'

he said with an expressive roll of his eyes. 'People will think it highly unusual if within hours of the ceremony we go our separate ways. That's not how newly married couples behave.'

'But what about Scraps?' she asked. 'I can't just leave him. I've only just got him to trust me. He probably won't take food off Franco or Elena. He might starve or run away again.' She narrowed her gaze at him pointedly and added, 'Or get shot.'

Andreas let out a breath. 'Is that mangy-looking mongrel really that important to you?'

'Yes,' Sienna said. 'I've never had a pet before. I was never allowed to have one because we always lived in a flat or other people's houses. I've always wanted my own dog. Dogs don't judge you. They love you no matter how little or much money you have and they don't give a toss about whether or not you come from a posh suburb or a trailer park. I've always wanted to be…' She suddenly checked herself. God, how embarrassing. What was she thinking, blurting out all those heartfelt longings as if she was a soppy fool?

Andreas was looking at her quizzically. It

was the sort of look that suggested he was seeing much more than she wanted him to see.

Sienna lifted a shoulder in an indifferent shrug as she took another sip of her wine. 'Now that I think of it, maybe Elena could toss him a bone or two,' she said. 'I won't be able to take him with me when I leave in six months, anyway. Best not to get too attached.'

'Why won't you be able to take him with you?' Andreas asked, frowning slightly.

'I want to travel,' Sienna said. 'I don't want to be tied down. I'll have enough money by then to go where I want when I want. It's what I've always dreamed of doing. Having no responsibilities other than to please myself. That's what I'd call the perfect life.'

'It sounds rather pointless and shallow to me,' he said. 'Don't you want more for your life than a never ending holiday?'

'Nope,' Sienna said. 'Give me nine to five partying any day, as long as someone else is paying for it.'

A muscle worked like a hammer at the side of his mouth, while his eyes had gone all hard and glittery. 'You really are a piece of work, aren't you?'

'That's me,' Sienna said, draining her wine glass before holding it out to him. 'Can you pour me another one?'

Andreas threw her a disgusted look. 'Get it yourself,' he said and strode out of the *salone*, snapping the door shut behind him.

The following morning Elena arrived earlier than usual to help Sienna prepare for the ceremony. She bustled about like a mother hen, gushing about how beautiful Sienna looked as she dressed in a slim-fitting cream dress, the purchase of which had hit Andreas's credit card a little more heavily than Sienna cared to think about.

'Signor Ferrante is going to be…how you say?' Elena said. 'Knocked out by you, *sì*?'

Sienna gave the housekeeper what she hoped passed for a convincing smile. 'I'll be glad when this bit is over,' she said, smoothing a hand over her abdomen. 'My stomach feels like a hive of bees.'

'Wedding jitters,' Elena said reassuringly. 'It happens to every bride.'

Sienna didn't feel like a bride. She felt like a fraud. She thought of her twin sister preparing for her big day with Emilio and she felt a twinge of something that felt very much like pain. When she was a little girl she had dreamed of a white wedding with all the trimmings: a church filled with fragrant flowers, with bridesmaids and flower girls and a cute little ring-bearer. She had envisaged a horse-drawn carriage and footmen just like Cinderella. She had imagined a handsome husband who would look down at her as he lifted back her veil with such love and adoration that her heart would swell like a balloon.

But then her dreams and reality had always had a problem socialising.

'Come,' Elena said. 'Franco has brought the car around. It's time to leave.'

Andreas was waiting at the foot of the stairs when Sienna came down. He hadn't been sure what to expect. He had wondered if she would appear in her signature torn denim or a ridiculously short skirt or even bare feet. He hadn't been expecting a vision in designer cream satin that was so stylish and yet so elegantly simple it quite literally took his breath away.

Her silver-blonde hair was up in a classic French roll that showed off her swan-like neck to perfection. Her make-up was understated but somehow it worked brilliantly to showcase the luminosity of her flawless skin. Her grey-blue eyes had a hint of eye shadow and her lashes were long and lustrous with mascara. Her model-like cheekbones were defined by a subtle sweep of bronzer and her lips adorned with a glisten of pink-tinted lip-gloss.

The only thing she lacked was jewellery.

An elbow of remorse nudged him in the ribs. He should have thought to buy her something but he had assumed she would spend up big all by herself since he had given her carte blanche on the credit card he had issued her with.

'You look magnificent,' he said. 'I don't think I've ever seen you look quite so beautiful.'

'Amazing what a bit of money splashed around can do,' she said in a flippant tone. 'You don't want to know what this dress cost. And don't get me started on the shoes.'

He took her hand as she stepped from the last stair, a smile tugging at the corners of his mouth. 'At least you're wearing them,' he said. 'I was wondering if you might go without.'

'Watch this space,' she said with a wry twist of her mouth. 'These are what I call car-to-the-bar shoes. They're not meant for walking unless you want to end up with seriously deformed toes.'

Andreas was aware of Elena and Franco hovering in the background, looking suspiciously like the proud parents of the bride.

In the space of a week Sienna had charmed them, along with the feral dog. She certainly had a way about her that was unlike any other woman he had associated with before. But then she was very good at fooling people into believing she was all sweetness and light, when underneath that friendly façade was a cold and calculating little madam who—like her mangy dog—could lash out and bite when you were least expecting it.

Andreas turned to Franco. 'Give us a few minutes, there's something I have to give Sienna before we leave.'

'Sì, signor.'

'Come,' Andreas said to Sienna, leading her by the hand towards his study. 'I have something for you.'

'God, my feet are already killing me,' Sienna said, click-clacking beside him.

'This won't take long,' Andreas said, closing the door once they were inside the study.

'Have you bought me a present?' she asked with bright interest in her eyes.

Another sharp elbow of guilt nudged him. 'No,' he said. He opened the safe and took out the box that contained a pearl and diamond necklace and matching droplet earrings. 'These are just on loan.'

'They're beautiful,' Sienna said, peering at

them for a moment before straightening. 'But if you bought them for your ex, then forget about it. I'd rather go without.'

Andreas lifted the necklace off its bed of maroon velvet. 'These belonged to my mother,' he said. 'She wore them on her wedding day.'

She looked at the jewels without touching them. 'I'm not sure your mother would appreciate me wearing her jewellery.' She raised her eyes to his. 'It seems a bit…tacky, given the circumstances, don't you think?'

Andreas rolled his thumb over one of the pearls as he looked at her. 'Every Ferrante bride has worn them,' he said. 'They are a family heirloom.'

'Oh…well, then,' she said, turning her back to him. 'That's different. I wouldn't want to break with tradition or anything.'

Andreas fastened the necklace around her neck, his fingers fumbling over the catch as his skin came into contact with the silk of hers. 'You smell nice,' he said. 'Is that a new perfume?'

'If you wanted me to stick to a budget then you should have said so,' she said, turning around to scowl at him.

Andreas handed her the earrings. 'I think

you've shown remarkable restraint,' he said. 'But then it's early days yet.'

She clipped on the earrings, still giving him the evil eye as she did so. 'There,' she said once she was done. 'How do I look?'

'Breathtaking,' he said.

'Good,' she said. 'It's not every day a girl like me gets to marry a billionaire. I want to make the most of every single minute of it.'

Andreas held open the door, his jaw set in a tight line. *Not if I can help it*, he said beneath his breath as she sashayed past him.

Sienna had thought her marriage ceremony to Brian Littlemore had been a bit on the sterile and impersonal side but it had nothing on the clinical detachment of the service Andreas had organised. The vows were nothing like the ones she had composed in her girlish dreams. They were stilted and formal and she'd even been forced to say the O word. Obey.

She was fuming by the time it was almost over. Her lips felt as if they'd been stitched in place. Her teeth were half a centimetre down from grinding and her back was rigid with tension.

'You may kiss the bride.'

The words jolted her out of her simmering fury. 'I don't think—'

Andreas drew her closer, one of his hands in the small of her back, the other holding the hand that had not long ago received the slim gold band that now bound her to him as his wife. 'Relax, *ma chèrie*,' he said in an undertone. 'This one is for the cameras.'

'What cam—?'

A flash went off but it wasn't from any lurking cameras. It was a flare inside Sienna's brain that almost took the top of her head off. As soon as Andreas's lips touched down on hers she felt a tectonic shift of her equilibrium. The world seemed to tilt on its axis.

His lips were firm and yet soft.

Warm and yet dry.

He tasted of…she wasn't quite sure. It was something she had never tasted before and yet it was incredibly addictive.

She wanted more.

She *craved* more.

Her hands went to the front of his chest. She could feel his heart thudding beneath her palm. It mimicked the erratic rhythm of hers. He felt warm and male and vital. He felt strong and capable and arrantly potent.

His tongue stroked along the seam of her lips, a bold and commanding stroke that didn't ask permission for entry, but rather *demanded* it.

She opened to him on a soft little whimper, her stomach dropping in delight as his tongue deftly found hers. She felt the stirring of his arousal, the hot, hard length of him swelling against her as his mouth wreaked sensual havoc on hers. She moved closer, an instinctive, almost involuntary shift against him that evoked a husky-sounding groan from his throat as he deepened the kiss even further.

'Ahem…' The celebrant cleared his throat. 'I have another ceremony in five minutes.'

Sienna stepped out of Andreas's hold, her heart still galloping like a racehorse on steroids. Her mouth was tingling, every nerve alive with feeling, her lips swollen and sensitive from the pressure of his. She ran the tip of her tongue over them and tasted his hot male potency. Her stomach gave another tripping movement as she looked up at his darkly hooded gaze…

A flash went off but this time it was the surge of the paparazzi.

'Looks like it's show time,' Andreas said grimly and, taking her hand in his, led her towards the pack of journalists and photographers.

* * *

Sienna's emotions were in such turmoil she didn't want to examine them too closely. She had responded with such wantonness to Andreas. She had forgotten everything but the feel of his mouth on hers. The whole world had ceased to exist in that heart-stopping moment when he had kissed her with such fiery passion and intent. She had felt the primal rhythm of his blood through the surface of his lips. She hadn't wanted the kiss to end. Her insides were still trembling from the sensual onslaught of being in his arms.

It was at least an hour before they could escape. Her face felt stiff from all the fake smiling. Her head was aching and her feet were throbbing by the time they got back to where Franco was waiting for them in the car.

'That went remarkably well,' Andreas said once the partition between the driver and the passenger section was closed.

'You think?' Sienna bent down to prise off her shoes. 'Ouch! I've got blisters.'

'Elena will probably have an intimate dinner set up for us back at the villa,' he said. 'She's a hopeless romantic so just go along with it.'

'She reminds me of my flatmate Kate back in London,' Sienna said, closing her eyes and flinging her head back against the headrest in bone-aching fatigue. 'She thinks you're going to fall in love with me before the end of this and beg me to stay with you for ever.'

'I hope you put her straight on that.'

'I did,' she said flatly. 'She forgot to factor in the fact that I wouldn't stay on even if you paid me.'

Andreas gave a mocking laugh. 'If the price was right you'd stay.'

Sienna turned her head on the headrest to glare at him. 'Even you don't have enough money to buy me, Rich Boy,' she said. 'And, just for the record, I am *not* going to obey you.'

He gave her a supercilious smile. 'You just promised to do so in front of a legally appointed celebrant.'

'I don't care,' she said, throwing her head back and closing her eyes again. 'I am *not* going to bend to your will.'

'So what was that kiss all about?' he asked.

Sienna jerked upright in her seat to glower at him. 'That was your doing, not mine,' she said. 'I was all geared up for the hands-off clinical deal we'd agreed on and then you sideswipe me with a wedding kiss. That was low. That was *really* low.'

His look was smouldering, and it centred on her mouth just long enough to set her lips tingling all over again. 'It was a good kiss,' he said. 'I can see why you have the reputation you have. I was starting to think how it would feel to have those lips of yours on my—'

'Will you stop it, for God's sake?' Sienna hissed at him. 'My lips are going nowhere near your…your whatever. We're meant to be keeping this strictly to the terms.'

He was still looking at her mouth with that hooded dark gaze. 'We could always adjust the goalposts a little to suit our needs,' he said. 'After all, six months is a long time to be celibate.'

'It's not a long time for me.'

The words seemed to hang suspended in the air for a moment.

'How long is a long time for you?' Andreas asked.

Sienna felt the weight of his gaze but resolutely kept her head facing forward. 'How long is a piece of string?' she asked.

She heard him give a snort of derision. 'You have no idea, do you?' he said. 'Do you even know the names of some of the men you've slept with?'

'Not all of them,' Sienna answered with ironic truthfulness. 'Some men don't require a personal introduction before they sleep with you.'

Andreas let out a breath of disgust. 'You

are such a shameless gold-digging whore,' he said. 'Don't you have any self-respect?'

'Plenty,' Sienna said, lifting her chin. 'I could've settled for the deal your father set up, but I know you'll pay more to have what you want. And you want it. You want it so badly you'll do anything to stop me from taking it from you.'

His hands went to white-knuckled fists on the armrests each side of him. 'You'd better believe it,' he said. 'Don't say you weren't warned.'

CHAPTER FIVE

As soon as the car pulled up in front of his villa, Andreas wanted to head to the furthest reaches of the property to put as much distance as he could between him and Sienna. He wanted to regroup before she made him lose control completely. But for the sake of Franco and Elena's presence he was forced to play the role of devoted husband, which included carrying his new bride over the threshold of the villa. He could already feel his blood simmering at the thought of holding her against his body.

Sienna gave a little gasp as he scooped her up in his arms. 'What are you doing?' she asked.

'It's considered bad luck not to carry one's bride over the threshold,' he said and strode to the door being held open by his housekeeper, who was smiling broadly.

Andreas felt his skin grow hot and tight

where Sienna's arms had looped around his neck. Her right breast was pressed against his thumping heart and the fragrance of her alluring perfume teased his nostrils. She was lighter than he had expected and she fitted against him like a glove. He tried not to look at her mouth. Tried not to remember how it had felt to taste her moist hot sweetness. The taste of her lingered on his tongue; it was a potent potion as addictive as a drug. One taste was not going to be enough. It was never going to be enough. But then he had always known that. He had fought it for so long. This raw need to have her as his had been a part of his life for so long he had no idea how to subdue it. It was an ache that resided deep within him. It would not go away, no matter how much he distracted or disciplined himself.

He wanted her.

He lowered her to the floor by sliding her down the length of his body, his blood roaring in response to her curves as they brushed against him.

He wanted her and he would have her.

He heard the soft intake of her breath and saw the flare of her pupils as her eyes meshed with his. The barrier of their clothes was no barrier at all. They might as well have been standing there naked.

Sienna glowered up at him. 'Was that really necessary?'

'But of course,' Andreas said. 'Elena and Franco were watching.'

'Yeah, well, no one's watching now,' she said. 'Let's just step back into our true characters and tear strips off each other again.'

He gave a soft deep chuckle and pressed her even closer with his hand on the shapely curve of her bottom. 'Why the hurry, *ma petite*?' he said. 'I'm getting to like the feel of you against me. You like it too, *si*?'

Her eyes were pools of stormy grey and blue. 'This is not part of the plan,' she said, but she didn't do anything to push him away. If anything her body shifted closer, a subtle movement that sent another hot lightning rod of lust straight to his groin.

'Is it not?' he asked with a mocking smile. 'You've planned this from the start. You want me to think twice about ending this marriage when the time is up.' He captured one of her hands and pressed his lips to each and every fingertip, watching as her eyes darkened with desire. 'And what better way than to entice me into your bed as soon as you can?'

Her gaze flicked to his mouth, her tongue sweeping over her lips. 'That's not what I'm planning at all,' she said in a breathless voice.

'I don't want to be married to you any longer than I have to be.'

Andreas's fingers tightened on hers. Her hand was dainty and small in the grasp of his. He could have broken her fingers with just the slightest pressure. He was so close to her he could feel her body warmth radiating through him. She smelt of summer, of jasmine and honeysuckle and red-hot temptation. The skin of her hand was soft against the roughness of his. He felt her fingers move experimentally against the cup of his palm, whether to test his hold or tease him, he wasn't quite sure. It shouldn't have had anywhere near the sensual impact it had. It felt as if she had dipped her hand down the front of his trousers and touched him flesh on flesh.

He brought his mouth down to hers for the second time that day, and for the second time in his life a seismic shift knocked him sideways.

She tasted of sweet, hot, forbidden longings. He couldn't get enough of her delicious moistness. He fed off her with a greed he hadn't known existed. He savaged her mouth like a hungry beast on a rampage.

It was rapacious. It was primitive. It was raw male lust let off the leash. He hadn't realised how out of control a kiss could get until he thrust through the seam of her lips in search of her tongue.

Hers was hot and moist and brazen. It danced with his in a tango that was as sexy as anything he had ever experienced. It shot fireworks off in his head. Desire filled him so tightly he thought he would explode. His teeth scraped against hers. She bit him and he bit her back. It only made him want her more.

He thrust a hand at the back of her head, his fingers burying deep into her scalp as he explored her mouth with a thoroughness that left both of them breathless. His hand found her breast. It filled his palm with sensual heat, the tight bud of her nipple pressing against him. She felt so damn good, so feminine and soft. His need pulsed and pounded against her belly.

He wanted her naked.

He wanted to see her silky skin, every gorgeous inch of it. He wanted to taste her feminine heat, to move his lips and tongue against her to make her scream with ecstasy. He wanted to drive himself deep within her honeyed warmth, to feel the tight grip of her body contracting around him as she came.

He started to lift up the skirt of her dress but she suddenly stepped back, turning away from him with her arms going across her body as if she were suffering a chill. 'I'm sorry, Andreas,' she said. 'I don't want to continue with this.'

'Is this part of your technique?' Andreas asked. 'To tempt and to tease?'

Her cheeks flushed with delicate colour. 'It was unfair of me to give you the wrong impression,' she said. 'I didn't mean to mislead you.'

'The impression you gave me is that you want me just as much as I want you,' he said.

'Yes, well, I'm sorry about that but I had no idea that was going to happen every time you kiss me,' she said with a return to her haughty air. 'Maybe you should keep your mouth to yourself for the rest of the time we have together.'

'Ah, but that would not be half as much fun, would it, *ma belle*?' he asked. 'I quite like kissing you. I am developing rather a hunger for it, actually.'

She challenged him with those incredible grey-blue eyes and that stubborn little up-tilted chin. 'Then you'll have to satisfy your appetite elsewhere. I'm not going to be a rich man's mistress.'

'You're not my mistress,' he said. 'You're my wife.'

'Same difference, as far as I can see,' she threw back.

Andreas fought down his frustration and anger. She had been toying with him all along and he had been fool enough to fall for it. She knew how much he wanted her. It wasn't as if he could hide it. She had sensed it. Damn it, she had *felt* it.

And she wanted him. He'd have to be blind not to see it. He felt it in her kiss, in her touch and in the way she had pressed herself closer as if she had wanted to climb into his skin.

He would not rest until he had her where he wanted her.

Where he had always wanted her.

Sienna was the one woman who could make him lose all sense of control. He had sensed it all those years ago and had fought it determinedly.

But now was different.

Now there was nothing to stop them exploring the heat and passion that was flaring between them every time they were in the same room.

He could hardly wait.

Sienna closed her bedroom door and leant back against it, her heart thumping like a jackhammer. Her breathing was still out of

control and her insides quivered with a longing so intense she could barely stand up. They
had been married only a matter of a couple
of hours and already things were spinning
dangerously out of control. She didn't want
to feel this level of attraction, not to Andreas
Ferrante, not to a man who hated her as much
as he desired her. But what was she to do?
Her mind said *no* but her body kept saying
a resounding *yes*. It completely disregarded
her common sense. Instead, it was set on a
pathway to sensual hedonism that she could
not control. She didn't want to end up like her
mother, madly in love with a man who only
saw her as a convenient outlet for his lust.
Unrequited love for Andreas's father had destroyed her mother. After Guido Ferrante had
rejected her so publicly, Nell had sunk into
an alcohol and prescriptions drugs binge that
had eventually killed her.

Sienna wasn't prepared to go down the
same path of destruction. She was determined
to keep her heart well guarded. Andreas was
by far the most attractive man she had ever
met and his kisses were a temptation she
couldn't seem to resist, but that didn't mean
she had to fall in love with him. She had
thought herself in love with him as a teenager,
but that had just been a youthful crush, an in-

fatuation that had got totally out of hand. She was no longer that foolish star-struck teenager caught up in the fantasy of thinking a well-born rich and powerful man was the answer to all of her problems.

Things would be different this time.

She would do what other young women her age did and what men had been doing for centuries. She would separate her emotions from her physical needs. Sex would be just sex. Love would not come into it at all.

Sienna joined Andreas in the *salone* for the intimate celebration Elena had taken such delight in setting up for them. The housekeeper was clearly in her element, a beaming smile was spread across her face as she brought in an ice bucket and a bottle of vintage champagne.

'I have left everything ready for you in the dining room,' she said. 'You will prefer to be alone, *sì*? It will be much more romantic.'

'*Grazie*, Elena,' Andreas said. 'I'm sure it will be delightful.'

'Thank you for going to so much trouble,' Sienna chimed in. 'I saw the dining room on my way past. It looks fabulous with all the candles and the food smells absolutely delicious.'

'Enjoy,' Elena said and bustled out, closing the door softly as she left.

Sienna went over to where Andreas was standing and handed him his mother's pearl necklace and earrings. 'I thought I'd better hand these back before I get too attached to them,' she said. 'I'm sure your next bride will appreciate the chance to carry on the tradition.'

He took them from her with an unreadable expression on his face. 'Thank you,' he said.

'So,' she said with forced brightness. 'Champagne, huh?'

'Yes,' he said. 'Would you like some?'

'Why not?'

Sienna watched as he unpeeled the foil cover and unwound the wire before he popped the cork. A soft flutter like wings passed over the floor of her belly as she thought of those hands on her breasts and other parts of her anatomy. He had beautiful hands. Not soft and unused to hard work, but strong and capable.

She took the bubbling glass of champagne from him and was about to take a sip when his voice stalled her.

'Shouldn't we make a toast?'

'Sure,' she said, holding her glass up. 'What shall we drink to?'

He clinked his glass against hers, his eyes holding hers in a steely little lockdown that made her spine tingle. 'To making love, not war.'

She looked at him archly. '*Love*, Andreas?' she said. 'Don't you mean sex?'

His eyes glinted smoulderingly as he gave her a half-smile. 'You want it as much as I do,' he said. 'There's no point pretending otherwise.'

Sienna gave a little indifferent shrug. 'I admit the thought of seeing what you're like in bed holds a certain fascination,' she said. 'But I don't want you getting any ideas that *if* we conduct an intimate relationship it will mean anything to me other than the satiation of physical lust.'

He held her gaze for a pulsing moment. 'If?'

She gave him a defiant look. 'If.'

He took a leisurely sip of his champagne. 'I think we both know this thing between us is not going to go away,' he said. 'The thing is, it can only last as long as six months. By that time we will both have achieved what we want and will be free to move on with our lives.'

Sienna toyed with the champagne flute with her fingers, determined to rattle his chain as much as she could. It was an impish urge in her she couldn't quite control. 'What if you want me to stay a little longer?' she asked. 'What if you get so used to having me around you don't want to let me go?'

His hazel eyes drilled into hers with burning intensity. 'I will let you go, Sienna,' he said. 'Make no mistake about that. You are not the woman I want to be my wife or the future mother of my children.'

Sienna wasn't expecting his cutting response to hurt, but it had and deeply. Having children of her own was a subject she had put to the back of her mind. It was one of those things she didn't want to think about. Her childhood had been so unsettled and chaotic, and her mother's example of mothering so poor, she had always felt worried she might not be a good mother herself. But to hear Andreas say she was a totally unsuitable candidate as the mother of his children made her feel crushed in that closely guarded centre of her being. No woman wanted to hear that sort of insult. It felt as if she had been stabbed in the heart. The pain was so acute and so raw it momentarily took her breath away. She was annoyed at herself for feeling so upset. It wasn't like her to be so emotionally ambushed by a throwaway comment.

She quickly disguised her feelings by pasting an insolent smile on her face. 'Just as well, because I'm not planning on ruining my figure any time soon for a brood of obnoxious brats,' she said. 'Even a billionaire's ones.'

Andreas's eyes hardened. 'Is your twin sister as selfish and shallow as you?' he asked.

Sienna took a sip of her champagne. 'You can find out for yourself when you meet her in a few weeks,' she said. 'I'm going to be her bridesmaid. You'll be expected to attend the wedding with me in Rome. Won't that be fun?'

'I can hardly wait,' he said dryly.

Sienna sat down and flung one leg over the other, idly swinging her ankle up and down. 'So, this proposed honeymoon,' she said. 'When do we leave?'

'Tomorrow morning,' he said. 'I can only be away a couple of days, three at the most. I have a lot of work on at the moment.'

'Is it absolutely necessary I come with you?' she asked.

'We've already had this discussion, Sienna,' he said a little impatiently. 'I'm sure your dog will survive the separation from you. I have already spoken to Franco about making sure it is taken care of.'

She gave him a narrow-eyed look. 'You're

not going to get rid of him while my back is turned, are you?'

'While I don't share your enthusiasm for the mutt, I can see you've taken him on as some type of project,' he said. 'I just hope you won't be disappointed when he fails to live up to your expectations. He's half wild and quite possibly dangerous. You shouldn't let your guard down around him in case he reverts to form.'

'You sound as if you care about my welfare, Andreas,' Sienna said giving him a teasing smile. 'How touching.'

Andreas put his barely touched drink down. 'We should go and eat,' he said. 'I don't want the food to be spoiled.'

While the wedding ceremony had not been in line with Sienna's dreams, the wedding breakfast Andreas's housekeeper had prepared certainly was. Dish after delectable dish of local produce had been laid out in the dining room. There were hot dishes and cold ones, main ones and gorgeous desserts. Elena had even made a wedding cake. It was only a small one but it had been decorated with marzipan and white royal icing with fresh flowers as decoration. It even had a bride and groom on the top, and a silver knife with a satin ribbon tied around the handle lay ready.

It was a jarring reminder that none of this was for real.

'Gosh, will you check this out,' Sienna said. 'Elena's made us a wedding cake. Isn't that sweet?' She leaned down to peer at the plastic figures standing together. 'And the groom even looks like you, see? He looks all stiff and formal.'

Andreas gave her an irritated look. 'She shouldn't have gone to so much trouble.'

'No point complaining,' Sienna said as she picked up a plate. 'You're the one who insisted on telling everyone this is the real deal.'

'And what would you have done in my place?' he asked in an embittered tone. 'Told everyone you know—including the world's media—that you've been manipulated by your father into marrying a sleep-around gold-digging slut? I would be laughed out of town, if not the country.'

The words echoed in the silence.

Sienna put the plate she was holding down on the sideboard with calculated precision in case she was tempted to throw it at his face. Then, turning to face him, she gave him the coldest look she could muster. 'Enjoy your dinner,' she said. 'I hope it damn well chokes you.'

She moved past him to leave but he blocked her with his body. 'Sienna,' he said.

Sienna refused to even look at him. 'Get out of my way,' she said through tight lips. 'I don't want to talk to you.'

He put a hand on the top of her nearest shoulder but she jerked back out of his grasp. 'Don't you dare touch me,' she said, glaring at him furiously. 'I can't bear it when you touch me.'

His green and brown-flecked eyes challenged hers. 'We both know that's not true.'

'It *is* true,' she said. 'I hate you. I hate the way you think you can just crook your little finger and get what you want just because you're rich and powerful. You can't have me.'

'I *can* have you,' Andreas said with steely conviction. 'I can have you any time I want. That's what you're frightened of, isn't it, Sienna? You don't like it that you want me. You like it when you're in the driver's seat, but you can't be with me. You can't call the shots with me, *ma chérie*, because I'm not playing by your rules.'

Sienna tried to get past him again but he made a roadblock with his arm. Her belly tingled when she came into contact with those strongly corded muscles and she immediately sprang back as if he had burned her. 'Move out of my way or I'll hit you,' she warned.

His mouth curled upwards mockingly. 'Go on, I dare you,' he said. 'Show me what a little guttersnipe you really are.'

The hair trigger on her temper suddenly snapped. Sienna flung herself at him. She felt the tornado of her anger and frustration propel her forwards with such force she surprised even herself. Her fist landed a punch to his abdomen but it bounced off as if she had struck a slab of stone.

She slapped at his face but his hand came up and deflected it with a deftness that was as swift as it was effective.

She tried to kick him in the shins but somehow his thighs were so close to hers all she could do was make little shuffling movements with her feet that did nothing other than remind her how seriously outmatched she was.

There was only one avenue left and it wasn't one she normally used. She couldn't even understand why she was using it now. It bubbled up from nowhere, catching her off guard. Emotions she normally hid under layers of sass and cheek suddenly rose to the surface. She burst into tears but, thank God, it worked like a charm.

Andreas dropped his hold as if she were on fire. 'What the hell?' he said.

Sienna knew she wasn't the prettiest crier on the planet. Not only did her nose go bright red but it streamed as well, and her eyes got pink and swollen, and if she really got going she couldn't speak past the hiccups.

'Sienna,' he said, taking her by the upper arms. 'Stop it. Stop crying. Stop it right now.'

'I...I can't,' she blubbered.

He let out a whooshing breath. 'I'm sorry,' he said. 'I pushed you too far. I can't seem to help myself.' He pulled her into the cradle of his arms, one of his hands pressing against the back of her head. 'Come on, *ma petite*. Don't cry, please. I didn't meant to upset you like this.'

Sienna should have pushed back from him at that point but something about the warm, strong protective circle of his arms struck a chord inside her that insisted she stay right where she was. It felt good to have his heart beating right against her cheek. It felt amazing to have his hand pressed against her head in such a gentle and tender manner. It felt wonderful to have his other arm around her in a band of iron that made her feel safe in a way she had never felt before. His body felt so warm and solid. So dependable, so fortress-like she wanted to stay there for ever.

The breeze of his warm breath ruffled her hair when he spoke. 'This is not like you, *ma belle*. Has today been too much for you? I should have realised. You've had a lot to do to prepare. Leaving your flat and your friends in London, moving in with me and handling the press's interest in us. It's a lot to cope with in a very short time.'

Sienna gave a big noisy sniff and he dug in his pocket for a handkerchief. 'Here,' he said. 'Dry your eyes, *cara*.'

She buried her nose in the clean linen and pulled herself together with an effort. 'Sorry,' she said. 'I don't know what came over me. I don't do this normally.'

He brushed her hair out of her eyes with a gentle hand. 'I've been a brute to you,' he said. 'It's not helping anything, is it? We're stuck together and we have to make the most of it. It won't make the time go any faster by trading insults.'

Sienna rolled his handkerchief into a soggy ball in her hand. 'I'm sorry about hitting you.'

He gave a wry smile. 'I didn't feel a thing.'

She pressed her lips together, feeling a little more exposed and vulnerable than she cared for. 'Would you mind if I gave dinner a miss?' she asked. 'I think I'll have an early night. I have a bit of a headache.'

'Can I get you anything for it?' he asked. 'Some painkillers?'

She shook her head. 'No, I'll be fine. I always get a headache when I cry. It'll pass.'

She moved across to the door, stopping to turn to face him before she left. 'I'm really sorry, Andreas,' she said.

'You don't have to apologise,' he said. 'I was the one who was out of line.'

She chewed at her bottom lip for a moment. 'I'm not only talking about just now...'

His whole body stilled, as if every muscle and cell inside him had come to a sudden halt. His expression was like a mask, not even his eyes gave anything away.

It seemed a very long time before he spoke. 'Go to bed, Sienna,' he said. 'I will see you in the morning.'

Sienna slipped out of the room, closing the door softly behind her and, with a heart that felt like a dumb-bell inside her chest, quietly made her way upstairs.

CHAPTER SIX

DURING the journey to Provence Sienna could sense Andreas was making an effort to be polite and solicitous towards her. Whether it was for the benefit of any lurking press, or whether it was because he had taken on board her attempt to apologise for her behaviour all those years ago was still open to question.

Andreas had explained on the way in the car from Marseille that the chateau had been in his mother, Evaline's, family for generations, but since his uncle Jules had died some years ago without leaving an heir, the place had been left to Andreas's father in Evaline's will.

Although he didn't say anything specific, Sienna could tell Andreas was intensely frustrated that his mother hadn't changed her will before she'd died. Sienna knew for a fact that Evaline had found out about Guido's affair with Sienna's mother Nell several weeks before her death, but she had been desperately ill with aggressive rounds of chemotherapy. Sienna suspected Evaline hadn't had the energy or wherewithal to correct things before it was too late. She also suspected Evaline had been hopeful that her husband's affair was just a one-off thing that would soon pass.

As Andreas drove up the long entrance to the chateau, Sienna drew in a breath of wonder. She had seen pictures of the Chateau de Chalvy in the past, but it was completely different witnessing the exquisite beauty of the centuries-old chateau face to face.

Lavender fields lay in front of the chateau, while rolling green hills and pastures and the mountains beyond were its backdrop. A distant field of bright red poppies danced in the warm summer breeze. The air was fresh and fragrant and the birdsong from the shrubbery in the chateau's gardens was such a delight to hear after the bustle and busyness of the airport.

The tempting thought of actually owning this piece of paradise came back, but stronger this time. It dangled like an irresistible lure in front of her. If Andreas left her before the six months was up, all of this would be hers. Every hectare of fertile land, every ancient stone of the chateau and its surrounding buildings, every bloom of every fragrant flower and every blade of grass would be legally hers.

It made her heart thump excitedly. Was it mercenary of her to want a place like this? No one would be able to kick her out. No one would be hammering on the door for unpaid rent. She would feel secure for the first time in her life. She would have a roof over her head that no one could take away. It would be hers and hers alone.

But it could only be hers if Andreas called an early end to their marriage.

As Andreas was helping her from the car, the estate manager Jean-Claude Perrault and his wife Simone greeted them. The French couple were obviously keen to show Andreas that they were worthy caretakers of his mother's beloved estate, although their formality with Sienna was annoying. According to the Perraults, Sienna might be Andreas's wife, but she was a foreigner, and a British one at that.

After refreshments were served, Jean-Claude suggested he take Andreas on a quick tour of the property while Simone helped Sienna to settle in.

Sienna followed the Frenchwoman upstairs to where a suite had been specially prepared for their stay. Heirloom linen had been taken out of storage and washed and ironed, and the big walnut bed dusted and polished. Sienna didn't like to tell Simone that she and Andreas weren't actually sharing a room, so she just smiled and complimented Simone on the lovely décor and the fresh flowers sitting on the antique dressing table and on a chest of drawers.

'This has always been the bridal suite,' Simone said. 'For centuries, Chalvy brides have started their married life here. It has the best view of the lavender fields. It is a pity you can't stay longer. It is a very short honeymoon, but then Monsieur Ferrante is a very busy man, no?'

'Very busy,' Sienna agreed.

'I'll leave you to rest,' Simone said, some of her earlier formality softening slightly. 'Dinner will be served at eight-thirty. I have organised a chef from the village to prepare a celebratory meal for you both.'

'That was very kind of you,' Sienna said.

'Not at all,' Simone said. 'This is the first time in many years that Monsieur Ferrante has been to the Chateau de Chalvy estate. It is a time to celebrate both that and your marriage. Jean-Claude and I are happy he is finally settled. For a time we wondered if he would be like his uncle and never marry.'

'You mean Andreas's uncle Jules?'

Simone nodded as she smoothed the perfectly neat bedcover. 'He was very much a playboy,' she said. 'Definitely not a one-woman man, if you know what I mean. His sister Evaline, on the other hand, only ever had eyes for Andreas's father. She fell in love with him as a teenager. It was a happy marriage until…' She gave a discomfited smile, two spots of colour pooling high on her cheekbones. 'I should not be gossiping like one of the village girls. Forgive me. I forgot your connection to the family. I did not mean to offend you.'

'It's all right,' Sienna said. 'I understand my mother's involvement with Andreas's father caused a lot of pain for a lot of people.'

'I suppose no one really knows what goes on in a marriage other than the two people involved,' Simone said with a little sigh. 'Evaline loved Guido to the day she died, but I suspect he might not have loved her at all. Some men are like that, especially rich men. They can have anyone they want and they know it.'

Sienna couldn't have agreed more. Didn't her marriage to Andreas prove it?

* * *

'I have a problem,' Sienna said as soon as she found Andreas in the garden of the chateau. She had spied him from the window of their suite and had immediately come down to speak to him. He was standing on some flag-stones next to a fishpond where some frogs were croaking volubly. Water lilies floated on the surface of the pond and every now and again a flash of bright orange came to the top as a goldfish came in search of food.

'Let me guess,' Andreas said with a flicker of his signature mocking smile. 'You forgot your hair straighteners?'

She gave him a speaking glance. 'I am *not* sharing a room with you,' she said, 'especially the bridal suite. Do you have any idea of the trouble Simone has gone to? It's like she was expecting royalty to arrive. There are flow-ers on just about every surface and the linen your great-great-great-grandparents slept in has been brought out of storage and is on the bed, for God's sake!'

He took her arm and looped it through one of his and led her away from the fishpond to a long avenue of yew trees that led to a mag-nificent fountain. 'There are workers about, *ma chérie,*' he said. 'Keep your voice down.'

Sienna felt her breast brush against his arm and suppressed a shiver of forbidden delight.

'You have to do something, Andreas,' she insisted.

'There's no need to get all het up about it,' he said. 'It's only for a couple of nights. Besides, we can't break with the Chalvy tradition. Every new bride spends her first night there with her husband. It's been that way for hundreds of years.'

She stopped in her tracks and glared up at him. 'You knew about this all along, didn't you?' she said. 'You knew it and didn't warn me.'

'To be quite honest, I'd forgotten about the tradition until you mentioned the linen,' he said. 'My grandmother was the last Chalvy bride, as my mother married my father in Italy and only came back for occasional visits well into their marriage. And my uncle never married, so you are the first new bride to stay here since.'

'Aren't you forgetting a minor detail here?' Sienna asked. 'I'm not a Chalvy bride. I'm a Ferrante bride.'

Something moved at the back of his eyes as they held hers, something dark and pulsing. 'According to the tradition, a bride is a bride no matter who she belongs to,' he said.

Sienna narrowed her eyes at him. 'I don't

belong to you, Andreas,' she said. 'And you'd better not forget it.'

His lips curved upwards as he captured both of her hands in his and brought her closer. 'Stop scowling and start smiling like a blushing bride, *cara*,' he said. 'There's a gardener clipping a hedge about twenty metres away.'

Sienna felt the brush of Andreas's hard male body against her stomach and a flare of heat rushed through her. Her gaze went to his mouth, that beautiful, sinfully sculpted mouth that had already done so much damage to her equilibrium. It was impossible to ignore the way her body reacted to his. His proximity, his touch, even his hazel gaze sent an electric jolt of awareness through her. Her breasts rose to sensitive peaks against his chest as he brought her a little bit closer, and then her stomach plunged when he lowered his mouth to hers.

His lips were firm but gentle as they played with hers: a soft press, a lift-off, another soft press and then a slightly firmer, more insistent one. Then his tongue stroked over her bottom lip, making it tingle and fizz with sensation. She opened to him on a soft gasp and her stomach plummeted even further when his tongue masterfully took control of hers.

He cajoled it into an erotic duel, leaving her in no doubt who was going to win the sensual war in the end. He'd had her at his mercy from the first moment his lips touched hers. She was boneless within seconds, leaning into him, desperate to feel more of his magical touch…to feel the urgency of his need against hers…to feel the potency of his raw male desire. It made her feel dizzy with longing. The need crept through her like a stealthy opponent on a covert mission. She didn't want to feel so out of control but her body was hungry for every erotic feeling he was tempting her with.

He drove a splayed hand through her hair, tilting her head so he could kiss her deeper and longer, the rough stubble of his jaw scraping along her softer skin. She lost herself in the frenzied fever of his kiss. It was urgent, it was boldly insistent and, with that captivating edge of taboo about it, it made her forget about the past or the future. She was totally in the moment and the moment was all about him and how he made her feel.

His hand went from her head to slide down to the dip in her spine, pulling her against the jut of his erection. It was shockingly, shamelessly intimate. It made every sensible thought fly out of her head. She was suddenly and totally reduced to raw physical need.

His mouth lifted off hers as his gaze drilled smoulderingly into hers. 'Still want separate bedrooms?' he asked.

Sienna drew in a sharp little breath that was connected to something deep in the pit of her belly. 'I'm starting to see there could be some benefits to airing that musty old linen,' she conceded wryly.

He gave a spine-tingling chuckle as he cupped her face in his hands. 'I like how you make me laugh, *ma petite*,' he said. 'You don't kowtow to me like a lot of women do. I like that you are spirited and feisty. You always stand your ground with me.'

Sienna wished she could find some ground to stand on, but right now she was on the rockiest platform she had ever occupied. She was teetering on the edge of throwing caution to the wind and diving head first into a passionate affair with Andreas, no matter what the cost to her ultimately. She looked into his gaze and felt another layer of her resolve peel away like a slough of old useless skin.

She wanted him.

She had *always* wanted him.

She could have him for six months.

The thought was more than a temptation.

It was a statement of intent. The rationalisations began in her head. It was a finite time. She would be able to walk away when it was over. She knew the rules from the outset and so did he. It was a convenient arrangement, a no-strings affair that had benefits for them both. She wouldn't fall in love with him and he wouldn't fall in love with her. It would be an exciting erotic interlude to pass the time while they were shackled together in marriage. God knew she could do with the experience of a red-hot affair. Her body was craving an outlet for the sensuality denied her for so long.

Andreas stroked the broad pad of his thumb over Sienna's bottom lip, his hazel eyes meshing with hers in simmering heat. 'You know how much I want you,' he said. 'You've known it from the start. I think my father must have known it too, otherwise why would he have orchestrated this?'

Sienna salved her tingling lips with a quick darting sweep of her tongue. 'I meant what I said last night,' she said. 'I'm sorry I acted the way I did when I was seventeen. I panicked when your father came in. I didn't want my mother to lose her job. It was the first time I'd seen her really happy. I didn't want to be the one who wrecked everything for her. I didn't think things would get so out of hand. I didn't think you would leave and never come back.'

'There were lots of reasons I didn't come back,' he said, dropping his hands from her face to walk with her back towards the chateau. 'My father and I always had a difficult relationship. We locked horns on many things. He didn't want me to pursue my furniture design work. But I wanted to work for my wealth, not simply inherit it from him and his father and grandfather before him. I wanted to make my own way, not stand on anyone's shoulders. My father took that as a slight. He liked to have control, but I refused to play by his rules.'

Sienna walked alongside him, wondering if he would ever forgive her for her shameless behaviour. She had made his already strained relationship with his father so much worse. No wonder he hated her so much. She had ruined any chance of him making peace before his father had died. How could she expect him to overlook that as just a bit of immaturity on her part? 'I didn't realise the reason my mother was so happy was because she was having an affair with your father,' she said after a little silence. 'I think I would've acted differently if I'd known about that at the time.'

He stopped walking and turned to look down at her, an embittered frown slicing between his dark brows. 'Your mother wanted a quick leg up in life,' he said. 'She ruthlessly set her sights on my father. He was to be her next meal ticket. To this day I don't understand why he was so foolish to get involved with a shameless slut like her.'

'My mother loved him,' Sienna said, glaring at him for painting such a tawdry picture of her mother. 'He was the only man she had ever loved. She told me a few days before she died. Her life before that had been a litany of meaningless affairs. But once she met your father she fell deeply in love. She was devastated when he refused to acknowledge her publicly. I think she thought after your mother passed away that he would marry her.'

Andreas's expression was cynical. 'Are you sure it was him she loved or the lifestyle he could give her?' he asked.

Sienna gave him another flinty glare. 'I don't expect you to understand what love feels like,' she said. 'You're exactly like your father in that sense. You take what you want from people and give nothing back. Emotion doesn't come into it. Your life is a series of cold, hard business deals conducted one after the other.'

'Ah, but is that not just like you?' Andreas asked with a sardonic slant to his mouth. 'You married Brian Littlemore for money. You have married me for exactly the same reason. Is that not rather cold and businesslike? You want money in exchange for your body, but you will not give your heart.'

'Do you *want* my heart, Andreas?' she asked with a deliberately taunting look.

His gaze ran over her like the scorching stroke of a naked flame. 'I think you know what I want,' he said. 'It's what we both want. And tonight there is nothing to stop us from having it.'

She lifted her chin at him. 'I haven't said I'll sleep with you.'

He bent his head and pressed a brief but scaring kiss to her mouth. 'Not yet, but you will,' he said, flashing one of his satirical smiles. 'You won't be able to help yourself.'

'Let's see about that, shall we?' she said.

He touched her cheek with a soft brush-stroke of one of his fingers, his eyes burning hers with the glinting fire of his. 'I can hardly wait,' he said and, with another mocking smile, he left.

CHAPTER SEVEN

SIENNA felt in an edgy mood by the time she joined Andreas for pre-dinner drinks downstairs. She had successfully managed to avoid him since their meeting in the garden but she had been aware of him all the same. She had heard him come upstairs to shower and change for dinner. She had imagined him standing under the showerhead as she had done only minutes before, his body lean and tanned, all rippling muscles and toned naked male flesh. Her stomach had triple somersaulted at the thought of standing there with him, of feeling his hard body dividing the softness of hers to claim her as his. Her body seemed to be intent on having what her mind tried so valiantly to resist. Her traitorous body was clamouring for more of his touch, for more of his kisses, for more flesh on flesh contact—for everything.

And Andreas—damn him—knew it.

Sienna entered the large *salon* overlooking the chateau's formal garden with her nerves jangling in irritation. 'Where are Jean-Claude and Simone?' she asked. 'Aren't they joining us?'

Andreas gave her a crooked smile that made his eyes glint. 'It's our honeymoon, *ma chérie*,' he said. 'Four's a crowd, don't you think?'

She averted her gaze and reached for the champagne he had poured for her. 'I can see why you wanted to secure this place,' she said to change the subject. 'It's very beautiful.'

'My mother loved it here,' he said. 'She wanted her grandchildren to grow up like Miette and I did, with both French and Italian cultural experiences.'

Sienna looked at the bubbles in her glass, trying not to think of Andreas's future children running about the chateau and its gardens. It was unsettling to think of him with some other faceless woman on his arm, a woman he had selected as prime wife material. Or maybe he would take Portia Briscoe back once his brief marriage to Sienna was over. But that thought was even more upsetting. The more she knew of Andreas, the less suited Portia seemed to be for him. Couldn't *he* see that?

'Was Miette upset that the chateau was left to you and not to her?' Sienna asked after a little silence.

'My sister was more upset it was co-inherited by you,' he said. 'She is worried you will do everything in your power to make me default.'

Sienna could see why his sister would feel the way she did about her. Their relationship during the time she had lived with the family had been fraught with tension. Many a petty or bitchy argument had broken out between them, which, to be fair, Sienna knew she was largely responsible for. She had been insanely jealous of Miette as the only daughter of the Ferrante dynasty. To Sienna, Miette was everything she was not. Miette had two parents who adored her, an older brother who was loving and protective towards her, and she had grown up with the sort of wealth that meant she never had to worry about anything other than what designer brand to choose over another. Like Andreas, Miette had been to the best schools and university. Miette had even spent a year at a Swiss finishing school before she'd moved to London, where she had met her now equally well-heeled husband. Miette's life was the dream life Sienna had always wanted for herself. 'What did you say to her?' she asked before taking a sip of her drink.

'I told her not to worry,' he said. 'I am well aware of the tricks you might feel compelled to play.'

Sienna shrugged off his comment. 'Well, you can assure her I only want the money,' she said. 'The chateau is nice and all that, but what would I do with a place this size? I'd have to sell it. I could never afford to maintain it. The heating bills in winter must be crucifying.'

Andreas took a sip of his drink, still watching her with his hazel eyes. 'Just so you know, Sienna,' he said. 'I will not be tricked out of inheriting this property. You can do the time the nice way or the hard way but, either way, I am not leaving until I inherit what rightly belongs to my family.'

'Fine,' Sienna said, throwing him a testy look. 'But the same goes for you. I'm not going to be forced out by your brooding, boorish behaviour or your bad moods.'

Andreas gave an ironic chuckle. 'You're a fine one to talk of bad moods,' he said. 'You've been spoiling for a fight from the moment you stepped in the room. I can see it in your eyes. They've been flashing like sheet lightning for the last five minutes.'

Sienna glared at him. 'Maybe that has something to do with your own chicanery in making sure I have no choice but to sleep in your bed,' she said.

'What is the problem with sharing a bed that is large enough to house a family of five?' Andreas asked. 'I bet I won't even notice you're there.'

She set her mouth. 'Just another nameless woman lying beside you, eh? Nice one, Andreas. You have such class.'

'Are you jealous?' he asked.

'Of course not!' Sienna gave her head a toss. 'It's just that I don't like the thought of you suddenly forgetting who's lying beside you. You might take liberties that I'm not comfortable with.'

'Take liberties?' He gave a little snort of amusement. 'You sound like someone out of a Regency period drama. What, are you worried I might see one of your naked ankles or wrists, are you? I've seen a lot more of you than that, Sienna, and you know it. So, too, did most of the cyber world when your little bedroom peccadillo was aired, so don't play the outraged virgin card with me. It just won't wash.'

Sienna turned away so he couldn't see the way her cheeks coloured up. She concentrated on drinking her champagne, desperately trying to appear cool and collected when inside she was anything but. She hated him for reminding her of that wretched event. How like him to needle her with her past, the past she wanted to forget about, the past she wished had never happened. She pretended it didn't hurt but it did. Every time she saw a photo or snippet about herself in the press she cringed in shame. How could her life have come to that?

'Dinner will be waiting for us,' Andreas said after a moment. 'I hope you're hungry?'

Sienna gave him one of her arch looks. 'It sure beats making small talk, doesn't it?' she said and sashayed past him to the dining room.

Dinner was a tense affair. Sienna knew she wasn't helping things by being prickly but she resented the way Andreas always saw the worst in her. He assumed she would try to wangle him out of his inheritance, but if it weren't for the money she needed to kick-start her life she would have already defaulted so he could have the chateau. She wanted to be free of him just as much as he wanted to be free of her.

Well, maybe that wasn't quite true, she

thought as she toyed with her glass. The physical fascination she felt for him was something that drew her to him irrespective of the ill feeling between them. She could feel the tension of it brewing in the air. It was an atmospheric change that occurred every time they were on their own.

Knowing he wanted her made her need for him all the harder to ignore. She could feel the traitorous pulse of it in her blood, the way her insides clenched every time his gaze encountered hers. Those tense little eye-locks unfurled something deep inside her until she had to look away or betray herself completely.

'More wine?' Andreas offered.

Sienna covered her glass with her hand. 'I think I've had enough, thank you.'

There was a ghost of a smile in his eyes. 'Always wise to know when to stop, *si*?' he said.

She gave him a direct look. 'Do you know when to stop, Andreas?' she asked. 'Or do you keep going just because you can?'

He sat back and surveyed her for a moment before he answered. 'I don't believe in losing control in any area of my life.'

She raised a questioning brow at him. 'Not even during sex?'

He continued to hold her gaze with an intensity she found both thrilling and unsettling. 'It depends on what you mean by losing control,' he said. 'If you mean do I lose myself in the moment of orgasm, then yes, that is exactly what happens.'

Sienna knew her face was hot. She could feel it. So too was her body. Just the thought of him losing control—*having an orgasm*—with her was enough to send her senses spinning all over the place.

'You're blushing, *ma belle*,' he said with a slanting smile.

'I'm not blushing,' she retorted. 'It's hot in here.'

He rose from the table and opened one of the windows, letting in the fragrant night air. 'Better?' he asked, turning back to face her.

Sienna felt the caress of his gaze. It touched her from head to foot, lingering on the upthrust of her breasts just long enough for the fiery combustion of her need to engulf her.

She felt the tingle of her flesh as he came towards her, his eyes still doing that erotic little tussle with hers, as if he was already making love with her in his mind, running through the images of their naked limbs entangled, their bodies joined in the most intimate way possible.

Her body shivered involuntarily. She could

almost feel his hard male presence inside her. It started as a tiny flicker and then it became a pulse that was like a distant drumbeat inside her, growing in intensity as each sensually charged second passed.

Sienna swallowed as he came towards her with slow but purposeful strides. Her heart gave a stumble as he stood right beside her chair, the tip of his index finger lifting her chin to face him. 'What are we going to do about this tricky little situation between us, hmm?' he asked.

She rose to her feet as if he had drawn her up by tugging on invisible puppet strings. Her body was within a hair's breadth of his, her insides coiling tightly with lust. 'I don't know,' she said a little too huskily. 'Ignore it?'

His mouth tilted in that sexy smile again as his thumb brushed over her bottom lip. 'Sounds like a good idea in theory,' he said. 'How do you propose we do that in practice?'

Sienna swept her tongue over her lip where his thumb had just been and tasted the salt of him. A shockwave of longing rippled through her. She felt the rush of her blood and the hot tingle of feminine want darted like an expertly aimed arrow deep inside her. 'I don't know,' she said, trying to keep her tone light and unaffected. 'Do you have any suggestions?'

His hazel eyes pulsed as they held hers. 'Just the one,' he said in a deep gravel-rough voice.

Her gaze drifted to his mouth and her heart gave another little tripping movement. 'I sure hope it's a good one,' she said so softly it was barely audible.

'It is,' he said and, taking her by the upper arms and pulling her against him, chest pressed to chest, he bent his head and covered her mouth with his.

His lips were neither soft nor hard but somewhere right in between. They moved with mesmerising magic on the surface of hers before he took things to another blistering level with the bold and commanding thrust of his tongue.

It was like a flame let loose amongst bone-dry tinder. The kiss was suddenly hot and hard and urgent, just as hot and hard and as feverishly urgent as his body pressed against hers.

His hands went from their grip on her upper arms to slide down to her waist, one hand slipping behind her to press in the small of her back to hold her against the heated trajectory of his body. She moved against him, an instinctive and utterly primal movement that signalled her rapidly escalating need for him.

His mouth explored hers with spine-tingling expertise. His tongue played with hers, teasing and flirting at first, but then with increasing demand as his desire to mate took hold. She felt it in his body, the way he hardened and throbbed against her. Her body responded automatically. It softened and melted against him, her desperate need to get closer taking over whatever objections her scrambled mind tried to put up.

One of his hands skimmed over her breast in a teasing motion that set every nerve beneath her skin on fire. She whimpered against his mouth, pushing closer, desperate to have him hold her, to caress her, to touch her, to brand her with his lips and tongue.

He continued to kiss her deeply as his hand came back, firmer this time, cupping her, caressing her through the thin barrier of her dress and lacy bra. It was like torture not to have him as close as she wanted him. But then, as if he read her mind, or her body, or indeed both, he slid the shoulder of her dress aside. His warm dry hand on the skin of her neck and shoulder made her flesh sing with delight. He pushed the strap of her bra aside and then lowered his mouth to her skin. She shuddered in response when his tongue grazed the soft skin stretched tightly over her collarbone.

She snatched in a breath when he pushed the lace cup of her bra away. Her belly clenched with a hard fist of desire as his warm breath skated over her naked breast before his mouth closed over her achingly tight nipple. Thousands of fiery explosions went off beneath her skin at that toe-curling caress. His teeth and tongue teased her into a frenzy of want she had never imagined possible. The sensation of having his mouth suck on her made the hair on her head tingle at the roots.

Sienna slid her hands up his chest to work on his buttons; one by one she released them, kissing each section of his hot salty skin as she exposed it.

He made a deep sound at the back of his throat as she went lower, his hands fisting in her hair as she got to his waistband. The jut of his erection tented his trousers and she boldly touched him, caressing the length of him, delighting in the feel of him as he shuddered in response.

He made another deep guttural sound and pulled her down with him to the floor, his mouth slamming back down on hers as he pinned her with his weight. It was a bruising kiss but she was with him all the way, nipping at his lower lip, her teeth tugging and pulling at him in a desperate urge for satiation. His tongue thrust and stroked, cajoled and teased and finally tamed hers. In between hot searing kisses he got her dress off and her bra and knickers in a wild tangle of fabric and limbs that made Sienna's heart race with excitement. She only got his shirt off and his belt. There was barely time for the application of a condom before her head snapped back on the carpeted floor as he drove into her with a thick, hard thrust that made her cry out in sharp and sudden discomfort.

He froze above her. 'What's wrong?'

'Nothing,' Sienna said, quickly averting her eyes from his. 'It's been a long time, that's all.'

He captured her chin and made her look at him. 'How long?' he asked.

Sienna caught her bottom lip with her teeth. 'A while...'

His frown deepened, making a criss-cross of lines over his forehead and between his eyes. 'How long is a while?' he asked.

She gave a little shrug, secretly holding her breath. 'I can't really remember.'

His eyes were narrowed in focus. 'You

mean it is a while since you slept with your husband?' he said.

Sienna found it hard to lie to him when she was facing him eye to eye. 'I never slept with Brian,' she said.

His face blanched, his eyes shrinking back in their sockets as if she had struck him across the face. 'What?' he asked.

'It was a marriage of convenience,' she said. 'Brian wanted a wife in name only. I wanted the respectability of marrying well. It was a mutually satisfying agreement.'

Andreas pulled away from her and got to his feet in an agitated manner. He zipped up his trousers and then snatched up his discarded shirt and handed it to her. 'Here,' he said in a gruff tone. 'Put this on while I get your things.'

Sienna slipped her arms through the long sleeves and wrapped herself in his warmth and smell. His shirt didn't offer the same dignity as her clothes would have done but at least it covered her nakedness.

She watched as he gathered up her clothes from the floor, his hands folding them with meticulous care when only minutes ago he had been all but ripping them from her body. His brow was furrowed with a preoccupied frown as if he was having trouble processing what she had told him.

He came back over and handed the tidy pile to her, his eyes meshing with hers. 'I hurt you,' he said, his voice grave. 'I'm sorry.'

'You didn't hurt me…not really,' Sienna said.

'Why didn't you tell me?' he asked, still frowning.

'Tell you what?' she said. 'That I haven't had sex in ages? You wouldn't have believed me. The press make it pretty clear I'm up for it with anyone any time. Why would you take my word over theirs?'

'Why do you let them write that stuff without defending yourself?' he asked.

She gave an indifferent shrug. 'I don't care what people think. I know what's true. That's all that matters.'

'Why didn't you have a normal marriage with Brian Littlemore?' he asked. 'He paraded you about enough times. You were always at some gala event hanging off his arm like a trophy. Was it really all an act?'

Sienna wished she'd kept her mouth shut. What was *with* her tonight? Such honesty and openness was totally out of character. Before she knew it she'd be spilling the beans on Brian's 'mistress', the male lover he had adored even before he had married his wife Ruth and fathered three children with her. It wasn't her secret to tell. She had promised Brian on his deathbed she would honour his decision to protect his children from the knowledge of his true sexual orientation. But she realised she would have to be a little more careful around Andreas. He wasn't the sort to be fobbed off and lied to. His sharp intelligent gaze saw too much as it was.

'I'd rather not talk about it,' she said, hugging her pile of clothes close to her body. 'Brian was good to me. I don't regret being married to him. He looked after me.'

Andreas screwed up his face. 'He had a mistress, for God's sake,' he said. 'How could you have so little self-respect to allow that to continue right under your nose?'

Sienna squeezed her clothes even tighter against her body. 'I told you I don't want to talk about it.'

He studied her for a long moment, his gaze narrowing slightly. 'You married him soon after the sex tape scandal, didn't you?' he asked. 'It was only a few weeks or so, wasn't it?'

She kept her expression closed. 'What of it?'

'What happened that night?' he asked.

'What happened that made you suddenly run off and marry a man nearly forty years older than yourself?'

Sienna couldn't hold his penetrating gaze. She stared at the middle of his chest instead. Her chest felt tight and heavy with all the regret she carried inside. She had made such a mess of her life and her sister's. Maybe it was time to air some of her guilt. To confess how awful she felt about what had happened. Why she felt compelled to confess it to Andreas was something she would have to think about later.

'I was out drinking with friends,' she said. 'The girls I hung around with were regular binge drinkers but I never let myself get totally wasted. But that night…I must have had more than I realised or not drunk enough water or something. I don't remember much other than waking up in some guy's hotel room. I didn't know who he was. He was naked. I was naked. I was so ashamed of myself. For the first time I started to feel like the slut the press had always painted me. Before, I used to laugh it off when they wrote something about me being a bed-hopper because I'd only had sex twice.' She gave a little humourless laugh. 'By today's standards, I'm practically still a virgin. But after that night

I felt like I deserved it for not taking responsibility for my actions.'

'Did you ever consider you might have been the victim of a drink spike?' Andreas asked, frowning.

Sienna tried to shrug it off. 'I did wonder about that but, even so, it was still my fault for being so careless,' she said. 'I should've chosen my friends a little more carefully. I think they enjoyed seeing me pulled down a peg or two. I was always the one who kept her head. That night certainly put an end to that.'

'Sienna,' he said heavily, 'you were a victim of a crime. Why didn't you report it to the police?'

'Who would have believed me?' she asked. 'Like mother, like daughter, everyone would've said. Anyway, I didn't know if a crime *had* been committed. The tape showed me kissing that guy and him kissing me and his arms and hands all over me, but there was no way of knowing if anything else had happened.'

Andreas let out a stiff curse, his hand dragging over his face again. 'I can't get my head around this,' he said. 'Why didn't you say something when the press named your sister as the woman in that tape?'

Sienna shifted her gaze from his. 'I didn't

know about any of that,' she said. 'As soon as I woke up in that hotel room I caught the next flight out of the country. I wanted to get as far away from it as I could. That's when Brian stepped in. I rang him in a bit of a state from the airport. We'd met at a function a few years before and really hit it off in a friends-only way. He was like a father to me, the father I'd never had. He offered me a safe haven. I didn't think twice when he suggested we marry as soon as possible. I wanted the respectability. I wanted to feel safe.'

Andreas lifted her chin up so her gaze met his. 'Why have you let everyone believe such scurrilous lies about you?' he asked.

Sienna could feel her carefully constructed composure cracking. She was used to acting all tough and resilient but it was hard to keep that façade in place when Andreas seemed so tender and concerned. 'Can we drop this topic?' she said. 'It's in the past. I'd like to leave it there.'

'Sienna, you can't just brush something like this aside,' he said. 'You've let everyone—including me—believe you're a gold-digging slut when you're no such thing.'

She raised her chin away from the pressure of his fingertip. 'I might not be a slut but I still want the money,' she said. 'That makes me a gold-digger, doesn't it?'

He stared her down. 'That's what you want everyone to believe,' he said. 'Why do you do that? What do you hope to achieve by making everyone hate you?'

'People hate a lot more easily than they love,' she said. 'It's just the way things are. I do it too. I'm good at it. Look at just now, for example. I was prepared to sleep with you, even though I hate your guts.'

He continued to look at her for a lengthy moment, those hazel eyes searching hers until her heart jumped and thumped behind the wall of her chest. He touched her cheek with his fingertip; it was hardly more than a brushstroke but it made every pore of her skin reach up on tiptoe to feel more of his touch. 'If you didn't hate me before, then you surely do so now,' he said with a touch of ruefulness. 'I was rough with you.'

Sienna swallowed a tight tangled knot inside her throat. 'It wasn't that bad,' she said, affecting what she hoped was a casual tone. 'Anyway, I probably should've said something.'

He gave a self-deprecating grunt. 'Do you think I would've believed you?'

She acknowledged that with a wry on-off smile. 'Probably not.'

'Do you know the man's name?' Andreas asked.

Sienna felt a ripple of panic roll through her. 'Leave it, Andreas, please. I don't want Gisele to be reminded of it all again. She's about to get married. I know what the press would do if you went looking for justice on my behalf. There's enough CCTV footage of me coming in and out of nightclubs to make me look like the biggest lush out. You know how lawyers can twist things to build a case for the defence. I just want to forget about it.'

'You can't keep running away from un-pleasant stuff, Sienna,' he said.

She hoisted her chin. 'I'm not running away,' she said. 'I'm moving forward, for my sake as well as Gisele's.'

He held her gaze for a moment before he tucked a strand of her hair behind her ear, as one would do to a small child. Sienna didn't feel like a child, however. His touch against the sensitive skin of her ear made her shiver with womanly want and need. She felt him inside her still, a tender ache where her flesh had been stretched by his hot, hard presence.

What would it feel like to have him totally possess her? To have him move inside her in the throes of passion? To have him lose control in the soft, moist cocoon of her body? To feel her own body respond to his in a rhythm as old as time?

The silence throbbed with the erotic tension Sienna could feel in her body. She saw it in the dark heat of his eyes. It smouldered there in the black ink spill pools of his pupils. She felt the slow burn of his gaze move over her face like a lighted taper, scorching her like a blowtorch when it came to rest for a tantalising moment on her mouth.

Her heart gave a swift hard kick against her ribcage. Her tongue came out to moisten the arid landscape of her lips. Her stomach lifted and fell a thousand feet as he brushed that same gentle fingertip he had used on her cheek over the surface of her lips, a faint movement that sent every nerve into a frenzy of want.

His hand suddenly dropped from her face and just as swiftly a shutter came down on his features. 'I think it's best for the time being if we keep our distance from each other,' he said. 'I'll sleep in one of the spare rooms.'

Sienna hid behind the screen of her sarcasm. 'Frightened you might get too attached now I'm not the bed-hopping harlot you once thought I was?' she asked.

He held her look with cool but implacable determination. 'I want this chateau, Sienna,' he said. 'I am prepared to do whatever is required to obtain it. Neither of us needs the complication of a relationship that to all intents and purposes has been thrust upon us for reasons as yet unclear. If it hadn't been for my father's will, I would never have considered you as a temporary partner, let alone a life one. I suspect you would not have considered me either.'

'You're spot on there,' she said. 'You're the last person I would consider spending the rest of my life with. Can you imagine the fights we'd have? You're so anal you get antsy when the tea towels aren't aligned.'

'And you're so chaotic you're like a whirlwind,' he said, but he softened it with a wry smile. 'I still find it hard to believe you came from the womb of a woman who made a living out of being tidy.'

'Yeah, well, she might have been good at tidying up other people's messes, but she wasn't so crash hot at sorting out her own,' Sienna said with a little slump of her shoulders. 'I spent most of my childhood wondering where we'd be living the next week. Mum would say or do something she shouldn't and the next thing I'd be packing all my things.

I lost count of how many schools I attended over the years. The time with your family was the longest we'd stayed anywhere. I didn't want it to end.'

Andreas took one of her hands in his, toying with her fingers, one by one. 'I had no idea things were so difficult for you,' he said. 'I always thought you were a bit of a brat, but now I can see why you flounced around with such an attitude all the time. You felt terribly insecure.'

'I shouldn't complain,' Sienna said, trying to ignore the sensations firing up her arms from the warm stroke of his fingers against hers. 'Plenty of people have it so much worse.'

He brought her hand up to his mouth and gently kissed her bent knuckles. 'I should let you get to bed,' he said, giving her hand one last gentle squeeze before releasing it. 'Is there anything I can get or do for you? Perhaps run a hot bath for you?'

Sienna could see the concern in his eyes. It made her feel delicate and feminine, a startling and somewhat unsettling change from having to act tough and streetwise around him. 'No, I think I can manage to turn on the taps for myself,' she said with a crooked smile. 'Thanks all the same.'

He continued to study her for a long pulsing

moment. Sienna suspected those green and brown-flecked eyes could see right through her shabbily erected façade. That brief moment of physical intimacy had changed the dynamic between them and she wasn't sure how it could be changed back. The air was thick with the sensual energy their brief but passionate encounter had unleashed. It swirled like a current, a wild vortex that could so easily carry her way out of her depth if she wasn't careful.

'What happened here tonight...' He frowned as if searching for the right words. 'I don't know how to make it up to you. I've misjudged you, misunderstood you and insulted you. I hope you will find it in your heart to forgive me.'

'Wow, I really like this nice guy thing you've got going,' Sienna said. 'Maybe I won't hate you quite so much if you keep that up for the next six months.'

His eyes pulsed with something dark and intense as they held hers. 'You don't hate me, *ma petite*,' he said. 'In fact, I have a feeling you have never hated me.'

She challenged him with another lift of her chin. 'You surely don't think I'm still harbouring that silly little teenage crush on you, do you?' she said. 'That was a long time ago,

Andreas. I might not have as much experience as other women my age, but I can assure you I haven't been saving myself for you.'

'Why haven't you got involved with anyone?' he asked. 'It can't have been for lack of opportunity. Men fall over themselves to be with you. I've seen it with my own eyes. You can stop a speeding train with your looks.'

'I saw my mother move from one shallow hook-up after the other,' Sienna said. 'I saw what it did to her self-esteem. I was always picking up the emotional pieces. I felt like the parent a lot of the time. I guess it turned me off the thought of allowing someone that close who could turn around and hurt you. Besides, I want to be appreciated for more than my looks. I have dreams and aspirations. I'm not a narcissistic airhead. Unfortunately, a lot of men can't see past the physical stuff, or maybe they don't want to.'

He moved his fingertips across the sensitive skin on the slope of her lower jaw in a soft-as-air caress that set her nerves into a frenzied dance. 'You're a complex little thing, aren't you, *cara*?' he said.

'No more complex than the next person,' she said, shooting him a look from beneath her lashes. 'And not half as complex as you.'

A wry smile tipped up the corners of his

mouth. 'Perhaps we are more alike than we are different, *sì*?'

'I don't think we have much in common at all,' Sienna said, barely able to breathe with his fingers tracing back and forth along the line of her jaw.

He trailed a fingertip over her bottom lip before dropping his hand back down by his side. 'Perhaps you're right,' he said as he moved over to open the door for her. 'Call me if you need anything during the night. I'll only be a few doors down the hall.'

She gave a vague nod and moved past him in the doorway, trying not to notice his warm body so close she could have touched it. 'Goodnight.'

The only answer she got was the soft, but no less definite, closing of the door.

CHAPTER EIGHT

ANDREAS paced the floor for hours after Sienna had left. Her perfume lingered in the air. He could even smell it on his skin. He could still taste the sweetness of her in his mouth in spite of the three stiff drinks he had consumed since.

The shock of finding out she had never had a sexual relationship with her late husband had left him more than a little dumbfounded. Just about everything he had believed about her was wrong. He had thought she had prostituted herself by marrying for money. To find the marriage had been nothing more than a paper arrangement had completely stunned him.

And that wasn't even half of it. He couldn't get his head around the fact that she had so little experience. She'd only had two sexual partners and she was twenty-five years old. For all these years she had played the role of a hardened tart. The press had constantly portrayed her as an easily picked up party girl and she had done nothing to discourage that view. The circumstances of the sex tape scandal had obviously affected her deeply, as indeed they would most young women. Andreas suspected she had hidden behind the label of gold-digger because that was Sienna's way of hiding her hurt, by toughing it out and pretending it didn't matter one jot, when of course it did.

Guilt gnawed at his conscience. He had pulled her to the floor like a common whore. Desire and lust had got the better of him. It had got the better of both of them. She had been just as willing, but it didn't make him feel any less responsible.

He had physically hurt her.

He groaned out loud and paced some more. He had acted *exactly* like his father. He had been intent on slaking his lust with no thought to the consequences. He dragged a hand through his hair. Was this what his father had wanted to teach him? To show him how hard it was to resist the lure of lust?

Had his desire for Sienna been so obvious? He had done his best to hide it. He had disciplined himself to ignore her on his visits or, at the very least, treat her as if she was just a kid. He had watched her bloom into young womanhood. From visit to visit she had morphed from a pimply fourteen-year-old to a sultry siren of ripe sensuality at seventeen. His rejection of her had been the honourable thing to do, and yet he wondered if that and not her mother's antics had caused her to hit the party scene in a defiant attempt to save face.

By the time she was eighteen or so she had a reputation as a wild party girl. A 'nightclub nymphet', some journalist in London had labelled her. Night after night she had teetered out of clubs and hotels with her gaggle of giggling girlfriends.

And then at the age of twenty-two she had suddenly married a man old enough to be her grandfather. Everyone had called her a greedy little gold-digger. He had done it himself. He had thrown the newspaper aside in disgust when he had read about it on one of his visits to England. He had sworn and cursed and called her every filthy name under the sun.

His chest tightened and cramped with its weight of guilt.

Sienna was nothing like the person he'd thought she was. For years she had hidden behind a façade to protect herself from being hurt. Behind that tough smart-mouth exterior was a vulnerable young woman, a young woman who had never felt safe and secure. He had made the mistake of assuming she was just like her mother, on the take for whatever she could get.

But Sienna was nothing like Nell Baker. She wasn't a social climbing harlot with no sense of propriety. Sienna had more pride than he had given her credit for.

Every insult he had flung at her came back to haunt him. She had thrown back her own insults with a feistiness of spirit he had always secretly admired. Defiance had glittered from her sparkling grey-blue eyes in every one of their exchanges. He had found it invigorating to spar with her. She always gave as good as she got. It was verbal foreplay. A little game they had played for as long as he could remember.

He closed his eyes as he thought of how she had felt wrapped so tightly around him. The silky warmth of her had engulfed him. His body still ached and pulsed with the burden of desire. It was a pounding ache that reverberated through his flesh.

He wanted her.

That desire was nothing new to him, but somehow now it was stronger than ever. He had tasted the sweet pleasure of her; it was like a drug he could no longer resist.

He drew in a breath and slowly released it as he looked out at the moonlit fields of the estate. Six months and all of this would be his. Sienna would get her pay-out and he would inherit what was rightly his.

He knew she wanted the money. She was currently out of work and the funds her late husband had left her were just about gone. He was confident it was enough to keep her by his side for the allotted time. An affair between them would be an added bonus.

He closed the curtains with a flick of his hand.

He had a feeling that keeping her with him was not going to be the problem. Letting her go at the end of the six months might very well prove to be the biggest hurdle he had yet to face.

Sienna woke the next morning to a knock on the bedroom door. She pushed the hair out of her eyes and sat upright. 'Come in.'

Andreas came in with a tray with fresh croissants and a pot of fragrant steaming coffee. 'I thought you might like breakfast in bed,' he said.

'Is this another Chalvy bridal tradition?' she asked.

His lips moved in the semblance of a smile as he set the tray down over her knees. 'One of many,' he said.

'Well, as much as I'd like to keep the ghosts of this place happy, I'm afraid there's no way I can drink coffee at this time of the morning,' she said. 'I'm a tea girl. Call me British if you must but, in spite of living all those years in Italy, I can't quite get used to starting the day without my cup of tea.'

He gave a little eye roll as he whipped the coffee pot off the tray. 'I should've guessed,' he said. 'Give me five minutes and I'll be back with your tea.'

Sienna tilted her head at him. 'You wouldn't last five minutes as a servant, Andreas,' she said. 'You have to accept all commands and requests with grace and poise.'

'Perhaps you could give me some lessons,' he said.

'You already know I'm absolute rubbish at following orders,' she said. 'As soon as someone tells me to do something I always want to do the opposite. I think it's a personality flaw or something.'

'I'll have to make sure I say the opposite

of what I want you to do then,' he said. 'It's called reverse psychology, *si*?'

'Something like that,' she said.

Sienna picked at one of the croissants once he had gone, licking the buttery crumbs off her fingers. She had slept fitfully last night. Her body had thrummed with need for hours, and then, when she had finally drifted off to sleep, she had dreamed of Andreas. She had dreamed of his mouth and hands pleasuring her, touching her, caressing her, of him making her body sing with delight.

She squeezed her legs together and felt that tiny intimate ache where he had been. It made her belly feel all fluttery, like a thousand moth wings moving inside her. She put a hand over her stomach, trying to stop the sensation, but if anything it intensified.

The door opened after a few minutes and Andreas came in bearing a pot of tea. 'Your tea, Madame,' he said with a bow.

'Way too obsequious,' Sienna said, smiling at him. 'Your employer would automatically assume you're pilfering the silver or something.'

An answering smile flickered in his eyes. 'Perhaps I do have an ulterior motive,' he said as he poured her a cup of tea.

Sienna took the cup off the tray, burying

her nose in the steam rising from its surface rather than meet his gaze. 'So I take it this breakfast in bed routine is a guilt trip, not a tradition?' she said.

'How do you expect me not to feel guilty?' he asked. 'I spent most of last night pacing the floor over what happened.'

Sienna kept staring at the steamy mist rising from her tea. 'You're making too big an issue out of it,' she said. 'Let's just forget it ever happened.'

He brushed a strand of hair away from her face. 'Look at me, Sienna,' he said.

She drew in a breath and looked into his eyes. Her belly did that moth wing thing again and her heart skipped a beat. His face was cleanly shaven. His breath smelt of mint. His eyes looked tired, however. There were thumbprint-sized shadows beneath them. Had he too spent most of last night wondering what it would have felt like to make love properly? Had his body throbbed and ached for hours as hers had done? Had he dreamt of her as she had dreamt of him? It was so hard to tell what he was thinking or feeling. He had never been one for showing much in the way of expression. She had only seen him smile a handful of times.

His fingers brushed against her cheek as

his eyes held hers. 'I overstepped the mark. I take full responsibility for it. I broke the rules we set down. It was a mistake I promise won't be repeated, not unless it's what you want. If you want a six-month affair, then, of course, I would consider it.'

Of course, Sienna thought cynically. She would be a convenient plaything to pass the time, just like her mother had been for his father. He would walk away when the time was up and leave her without a flicker of regret. Within months, if not weeks, he would go on to marry some other beautiful woman with a blue blood pedigree and fill his precious villas with his gorgeous little black-haired heirs.

How would she cope with it?

The same way she coped with everything else. She would put on a brave face. She would show him she could play him at his own game. She could be just as ruthless and mercenary as him. When the time was up she would walk away without a single regret, or at least none that he could see. 'I don't think an affair between us would work out,' she said. 'I think it's best if we stick to our original agreement.'

If he was surprised or disappointed by her response he showed no sign of it on his face. 'Very well,' he said, rising from where he had perched on the edge of the bed. 'I have some business to go over with Jean-Claude. I probably won't see you until this evening.'

'I'm sure I'll find something to amuse myself with,' Sienna said. 'Maybe I'll find a wolf or a wild boar in the woods to tame.'

His lips twitched as he looked down at her. 'I noticed your camera the other day,' he said after a moment. 'I thought you liked being in front of the lens, not behind it.'

'Yes, well, that just goes to show how little you know me, doesn't it?' she said.

His eyes held hers in a beat or two of silence.

'Does anyone know the real you, *ma petite*?' he asked.

Sienna gave a little shrug. 'I have friends, if that's what you're asking.'

'A person can have hundreds of friends but it doesn't mean anyone knows who they really are when they are alone.'

She gave him an arch look. 'Who are you when you're alone, Andreas?' she asked. 'Or aren't you ever alone? I bet there's always some willing woman to keep you company or some bowing and scraping servant to cater to your every whim.'

'It is one of the burdens of being born into wealth,' he said. 'One is rarely left alone.

There are people always keen to be with you, but it is never clear if they want to be with you because they genuinely like your company or because they want something from you.'

'Given a choice, I'd rather live life from your side of the tracks than mine,' Sienna said. 'Besides, who needs genuine friends when you have loads and loads of money?'

He looked at her unwaveringly for a long moment. 'Do you really believe that, Sienna?' he asked. 'Do you really think being rich will make you truly happy?'

'I'll let you know once the money drops into my account in six months' time,' she said, picking up the rest of her croissant. 'Mind you, I reckon a chateau thrown in for free would bring a smile to my face.'

His mouth flattened to a thin line. 'You are *not* getting the chateau,' he said.

'Lighten up, Andreas,' she said. 'I'm only joking. I don't want your precious chateau. It's probably haunted by all your stuffy old relatives anyway.'

'Try and stay out of trouble today,' he said, with his brooding frown still in place. 'And remember, if you speak to anyone, we're supposed to be on our honeymoon.'

She arched a brow at him. 'You're the one rushing off to work the first chance you get.'

He came back to stand next to the bed, his eyes raking over her smoulderingly. 'Changed your mind already, have you, *cara*?' he said.

Sienna felt those gossamer wings brush over her belly again as she brought her eyes up to meet his glittering ones. 'Not yet,' she said. 'You can't give me what I want.'

He cupped her cheek with his hand as his eyes held hers captive. 'What do you want, Sienna? A promise of forever?'

She forced herself not to blink. 'Of course not,' she said. 'Neither of us is the forever type.'

His thumb moved over the surface of her bottom lip. 'We could be good together for a while, *ma cherie*,' he said. 'It seems a shame not to take advantage of the situation we find ourselves in. You and me, alone and legally married. Why not explore the possibilities, *sì*?'

Sienna couldn't think when he looked at her like that. Those hazel eyes promised sensual heaven. That mouth had already tempted her beyond endurance. She wanted him even though she knew it would probably end badly. How long could she say no, especially after that deliciously hot taste of sensuality last night?

She drew in a breath as he brought his

mouth inexorably closer. The feather-light brush of his lips against hers made her senses skyrocket. The gentle pressure called every nerve into play, making her lips tingle and fizz like champagne underneath her skin. He lifted his mouth away but for a microsecond her lips clung to his. It seemed her body was determined to betray her, no matter what she said to the contrary. Need pulsed inside her. Rampant hungry need that only he could satisfy. She had always known it. He was her physical nemesis. No one came close to making her feel what he did. His touch, his kisses and his caresses all made her blood race through her veins and her heart gallop in excitement. She wanted to feel his complete possession. She wanted him to satisfy this aching longing that just wouldn't go away.

He gave her cheek a light brush with his fingertip, his eyes dark and intense as they held hers. 'Have you really only had two partners?' he asked.

'Yes,' Sienna said. 'I know the press have always made me out to be a sensual hedonist but, to tell you the truth, I felt awkward and uncomfortable having sex. I just wanted to get it over with. I didn't feel anything much at all.'

'That's probably because you weren't in

tune with the other person physically,' he said. 'The first few times you have sex you shouldn't rush it. You need time to get to know your body's needs and rhythm. I rushed things last night because I thought you were more experienced. It will be different the next time. I'll make sure of it.'

Sienna felt her insides tremble with anticipation. Could she risk everything to indulge in a red-hot fling with him? It would be a sensuous feast she could sustain herself with for the rest of her life. But could she keep her feelings well clear of it?

It was a gamble she felt more and more tempted to take.

'You sound pretty certain there's going to be a next time,' she said. 'Isn't that a little arrogant of you?'

'There's a difference between arrogance and confidence,' he said. 'I'm confident we're going to be dynamite together, but I'm not so arrogant to assume it's going to last.'

It wasn't quite the answer Sienna was looking for. It seemed to suggest he had only a passing interest in her. She was more of a novelty to him than a person of any lasting value. 'Does any woman hold your interest longer than a month or two?' she asked.

'Some more than others.'

'What about Portia Briscoe?' she asked. 'You were going to marry her. What were you going to do once you got bored? Have a little affair on the side, just like your father did?'

A flicker of heat passed through his gaze. 'My father made promises to my mother he later broke,' he said. 'I made no such promises to Portia. She knew what I wanted in a wife and she was prepared to provide it.'

'She's not the right person for you, Andreas,' Sienna said. 'Your housekeeper Elena thinks so and, quite frankly, so do I.'

His top lip curled. 'I suppose you think you're a much better candidate, do you?'

'No, but obviously your father thought so,' Sienna said. 'I can't see why else he would have done this. He must've wanted you to stop and think about what you were doing. Perhaps he didn't want you to lock yourself into a loveless marriage for the rest of your life.'

Andreas's eyes clashed with hers. 'So he locked me into a hate-filled one with you?'

'Only for six months,' she reminded him.

He looked at her for a long moment. 'You know, it was a whole lot easier hating you when I thought you were a money-hungry trollop,' he said. 'Now I know more about you, it seems rather unfair to maintain such negative feelings.'

'What are you saying, Andreas?' Sienna asked with a deliberately goading smile. 'That you're falling a tiny bit in love with me?'

'I'm no more in love with you than you are with me,' he said, his expression locking down like a shutter over a window. 'What we feel for each other is lust. There's no other fancy way of putting it. And, in my opinion, the sooner it burns itself out the better.' And, without another word, he left, clipping the door shut behind him.

Later that day Sienna was coming back from photographing the lavender fields when she saw Andreas in the distance. He was walking through the vineyard, inspecting the vines as he went along the rows.

She raised her camera and zoomed in to frame him in a series of shots. She captured him deep in thought. She captured him squinting against the late afternoon sun. She captured him picking a leaf from a vine and running it through his fingers, his brow furrowed in a frown. And then, as if he suddenly became aware of being watched, he turned and looked directly at her.

Sienna lowered the camera as he walked towards her. She watched as his long legs ate up the distance, the muscles of his thighs bunching with every step. Her belly gave an excited little quiver. He looked so arrantly male, dressed in dark blue denim jeans and a close-fitting white T-shirt. Every honed and toned muscle stretched against the fabric, reminding her of the potent power of his body. She had felt that hard male body move inside hers.

She wanted to feel it again.

He came and stood right in front of her, his towering height almost blocking the sun from her view. 'Are you going to let me see what you've been up to?' he asked.

Sienna positioned herself beside him and pressed the buttons on her camera to recall the shots. 'You make a good study when you're not aware of the camera,' she said. 'But that's like most people. It's hard to get a natural shot of someone when they know they're being watched.'

His eyes met hers. 'These are good,' he said. 'How long have you been doing this?'

Sienna shrugged dismissively as she turned off the camera. 'A while.'

He took the camera from her and turned it back on, scrolling through the archive of pictures she had loaded. 'You've got a good eye,' he said, looking at her again. 'Is this a hobby or is it what you want to do? To pursue a career in photography?'

Sienna took the camera from him, her fingers briefly coming in contact with his. 'I lost my office job when Brian died,' she said. 'His family didn't want me working in the business. It made me think about being my own boss instead of being at the mercy of other people all the time. Of course it will take me a while to build up the business, but I'd like to have a go at it. I could never afford decent equipment before. I'd need a much better camera for official portraits and wedding photography and I'd need to rent a studio. I couldn't afford to do that before. But after this six months is over...well, I'll be laughing all the way to the bank, won't I?'

His expression was deeply thoughtful. 'So why did you encourage me to think you only wanted the money for a layabout holiday and endless partying?' he asked.

She shifted her gaze from his as she put the camera back inside its vinyl case. 'I might not make it as a photographer,' she said. 'There's pretty stiff competition out there. I'm under no illusions that I'm any more talented than anyone else.'

'Where would you like to base yourself?' he asked.

'London,' Sienna said. 'But I could travel to other places on assignment. It'd be fun travelling around to take pictures all over the world. I could even do a book, you know, like one of those super-glam coffee table ones.' She flashed him a little smile. 'You could tell everyone you knew me before I was famous.'

'I'm sure you'll do very well,' he said, a small frown forming between his eyes. 'You seem to have rather a knack for falling on your feet.'

She tucked a strand of hair behind her ear that the light breeze had been playing with. 'What will you do with this place once you inherit it?' she asked. 'Are you going to base yourself here or Florence, or travel between the two?'

His eyes held hers in a brooding little lockdown. 'It is not yet certain that I will inherit it,' he said. 'It would be foolish of me to make plans at this stage. I'll take a wait and see approach.'

Sienna frowned at him. 'You don't trust me, do you?'

'This is a valuable property,' he said. 'It surely can't have escaped your notice that it's worth five or six times what you will get in the pay-out. Why should I trust you?'

'No, indeed,' she said, throwing him a blistering look. 'Why should you?'

He let out a breath of irritation. 'Sienna, I realise I've made some errors of judgement with you in the past, but I would be a fool to take it for granted that you'll abide by the terms of the will. We haven't been married a week. How do you know what you'll feel in six weeks from now, let alone six months?'

'I know exactly what I'll feel,' she said, glaring at him. 'I'll still hate you.'

'Best you keep on doing that,' he said, turning to walk back towards the vineyard. 'It will make the end much easier for both of us.'

'Why are we leaving so soon?' Sienna asked as Andreas loaded their bags in the car later that evening. He had given her very little notice. He had sent a message via Simone, telling her to pack as they were leaving to catch the next available flight. 'I thought you said we were staying for two or three days.'

'I've seen what I came here to see,' he said as he snapped the boot shut and came around to open her door for her. 'The Perraults are managing things just fine. I have other things I need to see to in Florence. I have a business to run.'

'Aren't you worried what the press will

think of you cutting short your honeymoon?' she asked once they were on their way.

He sent her a brief unreadable glance. 'I thought you were desperate to get back to your feral dog?'

'So you're doing this for me?' Sienna asked with a sceptical look. 'Somehow, I don't think so.'

'I'm doing it for both of us,' he said and put his foot down on the accelerator.

Sienna didn't see much of Andreas after they got back from France. Each day he left early in the morning and returned well after she had gone to bed. It annoyed her that he had just left her to her own devices, not even having the decency to communicate with her, other than via the housekeeper or a short text. It made her feel like an uninvited guest who was being tolerated, rather than welcomed.

But then, that was exactly what she was. Andreas had planned his life with meticulous precision. She had never been a part of it. She was the last woman he would ever have considered marrying. But his father's will had changed everything. So, too, had that brief moment of intimacy. Yet ever since that night Andreas had kept his distance.

Her heart gave a funny little spasm. He

could easily find someone else. He might have already recruited someone to satisfy his needs. There were hundreds of women who would do anything to be his mistress. Would she have to pretend not to notice for the rest of the time they were stuck together in this arrangement? Was he doing it to make her default on the will? After all, she was the one with the most to lose. All he had to do was wait it out and he could claim what was rightly his. Her lack of experience was probably the biggest turn-off for someone with his level of expertise. He probably couldn't wait to get rid of her now she was of no further use to him.

Sienna was sure Elena was well aware that Andreas didn't share a bed with his new wife, but the housekeeper was either too discreet or polite to mention it in any of her interactions with her.

Elena had mentioned something about a furniture design collection Andreas was working on, commissioned by a wealthy American businessman, and how it was taking up a lot of his time. 'He barely sleeps when he is working on a special project,' she said. 'He spends hours and hours at his office. Once it is finished he will be able to relax a little, *si*? Maybe he will take you away somewhere special for a proper honeymoon. It is lonely here all day on your own.'

'I'm not lonely,' Sienna insisted. 'I have Scraps to keep me company.'

Elena gave her an indulgent smile. 'It will be easier when you have a *bambino* or two to keep you busy, *sì*?'

Sienna pushed the thought of a dark-haired hazel-eyed chubby baby out of her mind. She thought instead of a home of her own in London, a luxury home with a studio and a garden and money in the bank—lots and lots of money.

That was her goal, not marriage and babies.

When Sienna came downstairs for dinner towards the end of the week Andreas was in the *salone* sipping an aperitif. His gaze skimmed over her coffee-coloured dress before meshing with hers. 'I was expecting you to send word via Elena that you wouldn't be joining me for dinner,' he said.

Sienna held her head at an imperious angle. 'I considered it, but then I thought that would be letting you off the hook,' she said. 'I'd much rather annoy you with my presence since you seemed to be actively avoiding it for the past week.'

A half-smile kicked up one side of his mouth. 'Feeling neglected, are we?'

She took the glass of wine he had poured for her, giving him a hardened look. 'Not at all,' she said. 'I just can't help wondering what your housekeeper thinks of our relationship, with you spending every minute you can at work while I'm stuck here twiddling my thumbs.'

'She is employed to keep order in the villa, not to speculate on my private life,' he said. 'She knows she would be fired immediately if she spoke out of turn. Anyway, if you're bored, why not take the car out I bought you?'

'I'm not bored,' Sienna said. 'I've got plenty to do; it's just I don't like having to pretend things are normal between us when they're not.'

'There's one way to change that,' he said with a glinting look in his eyes. 'We can make them normal. You can move into my bed tonight.'

Sienna felt her stomach do a flip turn. 'How can you be so clinical about this?' she asked. 'We don't even like each other.'

'Liking one another has nothing to do with it,' he said. 'Physical compatibility is what matters. I've had lovers I didn't like much at all, but they were perfectly fine as sexual partners.'

'Have you ever been in love?' Sienna asked.

'No,' he said. 'It's not that I don't believe it exists. I've seen it and admire it in others. I just haven't felt that level of attachment.' He took a sip of his drink. 'What about you?'

'I think my twin got all the love genes instead of me,' she said. 'I don't think I've ever seen two people more in love than Gisele and Emilio. Their wedding is in three weeks. You haven't forgotten, have you? I called your secretary to put it in your diary. I'm going to go a couple of days before to help with things. I'll meet you at the hotel.'

'No, I haven't forgotten,' he said. 'I'm looking forward to meeting them both, particularly your sister.'

'We're nothing alike,' Sienna said. 'Well, apart from looks, I mean.'

'You must have more in common than looks,' he said.

'Not much,' she said. 'Don't get me wrong. I adore her. She's so sweet and caring I can't help but love her. But because we haven't shared the same parents, or the same experiences, we want different things for our lives. I wonder if it would have been different if we had grown up together. I guess we'll never know now.'

He studied her for a moment as if he was memorising her features in fine detail. 'I wonder if I'll be able to tell you apart.'

'I'll give you a tip-off,' Sienna said. 'My sister will be the one wearing white and she'll have a big smile on her face. Oh, and a wedding band on her finger to match the fabulous diamond engagement ring Emilio gave her.'

'That reminds me.' Andreas put his drink to one side. 'I have something for you,' he said. He took an antique ring box out of his pocket and handed it to her. 'You might recognise it. It belonged to my mother and my grandmother before her.'

Sienna opened the tiny box to find the diamond and sapphire dress ring she had often admired on Evaline Ferrante's hand, nestled in the groove of black velvet. 'I do recognise it,' she said, looking up at him with a little frown. 'But shouldn't you be keeping such an heirloom for your future bride?'

'If you don't like it then I'll get you something else,' he said.

Sienna wasn't sure what to make of his expression or his curt tone. 'Of course I like it,' she said, putting it on her finger. 'I've always thought it was a gorgeous ring. But I'll give it back to you when we get divorced. That would only be fair.'

'Fine,' he said, refilling his glass. 'But I've noticed you don't seem to have a lot of jewellery.' He took a sip of his drink. 'What happened to all the diamonds you had dripping from you when you were with Littlemore?'

'I gave them back to his family,' she said. 'I didn't feel comfortable keeping them.'

He gave her another one of his thoughtful looks. 'I got the impression from what was reported in the press that his family never accepted you,' he said. 'At times they were quite vitriolic in their comments.'

'Yes, well, they loved their mother dearly and didn't want anyone to take her place,' Sienna said. 'I totally understood where they were coming from.'

'Do you think they would have accepted his mistress any better?'

She shifted her gaze from his. 'No.'

'And yet, by all accounts, he had been involved with her a long time,' he said. 'It seems strange he didn't offer to marry her instead of you.'

She shrugged off his comment and took a sip of her wine.

He continued to study her. 'You're very loyal to Littlemore, aren't you?' he said.

Sienna forced herself to meet his gaze. 'Why wouldn't I be? He was good to me.'

'There's more to it, isn't there?' he asked. 'It's been niggling at me for days. Why didn't he marry his mistress? Why marry a woman younger than one of his daughters instead of the mistress he had kept for all those years?'

'Maybe his mistress was already married,' she said.

Andreas lifted her chin with his index finger, locking his gaze with hers. 'That's not the reason, though, is it?' he said.

Sienna remained silent. The intense scrutiny of his hazel gaze made her heart beat faster and faster. It was harder and harder to hide anything from him. He seemed to see through the layers of her skin to the very heart of her.

'Brian Littlemore wasn't involved with a woman, was he?' Andreas said. 'His long-term lover was a man.'

Sienna swallowed tightly. 'That's not true.'

'Don't lie to me, *cara*,' he said. 'I hate being lied to. Don't you think you've told enough lies by now? Surely you can be honest with me over this. It will go no further than this room.'

She chewed at her lip. 'How did you find

out?' she asked. 'No one is supposed to know. Brian didn't want his children to find out. He was worried it would hurt them. He didn't think they'd understand. If this gets out in the public arena it will hurt so many people.'

'It's not common knowledge, as far as I know,' he said. 'I came to the conclusion myself so it's likely others will do so as well. But if it goes public, I can't see how you should be blamed.'

'Brian wanted to protect his family,' Sienna said. 'He came from a very conservative background. His parents would've disowned him if they'd known. He did all the things that were expected of him. He got married and raised a family. Even after his wife died he still had to maintain the lie. Do you know how hard that was on him? He was trapped. You mustn't let anyone know about it. You mustn't, Andreas. So many people will get hurt.'

He stroked her chin with his thumb, back and forth like a slow-moving metronome. 'You care more about his family's feelings even though they've trashed you any time they could in the press?'

Sienna looked into his warm hazel eyes and felt something reposition itself in her chest.

A soft little gear change of emotion that was totally unexpected and deeply unsettling. She didn't want to lose her grip on her feelings. She wanted to keep her emotions under lock-down. Falling in love with Andreas would be the biggest mistake of her life so far. She couldn't afford to let her feelings get involved. She had to be strong enough to walk away when the time was up. 'I care about what Brian wanted,' she said. 'He trusted me. I didn't want to betray that trust.'

Andreas's eyes held hers in an intimate lock that made her insides flutter. His thumb was still doing that mesmerising little caress that made her feel as if her nerves were pirou-etting beneath the surface of her skin. 'So you were prepared to let me carry on thinking you were a gold-digger?' he said as his hand fell away from her face. 'Does my opinion of you mean absolutely nothing to you at all?'

Sienna swept the surface of her lips with a quick dart of her tongue. 'I figured after this six months is up it won't be relevant what you think of me,' she said. 'We don't mix in the same circles. We probably won't see each other again.'

Something passed through his gaze as it held hers. 'That will be a shame, don't you think?' he said.

'Why?'

'Because I have a feeling I'm going to miss doing this,' he said, and lowered his mouth to hers.

CHAPTER NINE

Sɪᴇɴɴᴀ felt the warm, gentle pressure of his lips as they met hers. It was a slow kiss, no sense of urgency or out of control passion, just his lips moving at a leisurely pace as they explored the softness of hers.

She returned the kiss in much the same way, slow and soft, touching down, lifting off, touching down again, varying the pressure ever so slightly, but not the speed.

It was a getting-to-know-you kiss. It felt like a romantic first kiss between two people who were attracted to each other, but were mindful of overstepping the boundaries too early. A kiss where the two parties were taking tentative steps to see how well they worked together intimately.

No other parts of their bodies were touching. He didn't gather her to him. He didn't put his arms on her shoulders or her waist. She didn't put her hands on his chest or around his neck. Only their lips bridged the gap between them, but, even so, Sienna felt a roar of heat go through her. Her insides melted like the wax of a candle under a powerful heat source.

After endless dreamy minutes, Andreas slowly lifted his mouth away. His expression was faintly bemused as he looked down at her. 'You have such a soft, kissable mouth,' he said. 'It's surprisingly soft given how razor-sharp your tongue can be.'

Sienna couldn't hold back a rueful smile. 'Yes, well, you do seem to bring the shrew out in me at times.'

He made a little sound of amusement, a deep and totally male sound that made her belly quiver like unset aspic. His hand came up to cup her cheek, his thumb lazily stroking her skin as his eyes made love with hers. 'You haven't always brought out the best in me either,' he said. 'But maybe, once this period of time is up, we can walk away from this as friends. Do you think that's possible, *ma petite*?'

Sienna felt her breath come out in a little flutter but she hoped he hadn't noticed. 'I'm not sure I could ever get used to thinking of you as a friend,' she said playfully. 'I guess I'll have to find someone else to sharpen my claws on, won't I?'

He stroked her cheek one last time before dropping his hand back down by his side. 'I bet it won't be half as much fun with someone else,' he said, his expression now inscrutable.

Sienna had a feeling he wasn't just talking about their verbal sparring. The crazy thing was, she couldn't imagine kissing another man now. She couldn't imagine another man holding her and caressing her and making love to her.

She only wanted Andreas.

She gave herself a swift mental slap. He wanted the chateau, not her. She was a means to an end. In six months it would all be over. He would walk away from her, just as his father had done to her mother.

This wasn't forever.

'No, perhaps not,' she said. 'But I won't know that until I try, will I?'

His eyes flickered as if something behind them had momentarily become unstuck. 'We should have dinner,' he said, putting his glass down as if it had suddenly turned into a poisoned chalice. 'I still have some work to see to afterwards.'

'Do you ever take time to relax?' Sienna asked. 'You can't possibly go at this pace for weeks on end. It's not healthy.'

'I have a lot of people depending on me

for their incomes and their futures,' Andreas said, scraping a hand through his hair. 'My father's death couldn't have come at a worse time.'

'I'm quite sure he didn't plan to die just then to personally inconvenience you,' Sienna said in a dry tone.

'Don't bet on it,' he said with an embittered scowl.

'You didn't really hate him, did you, Andreas?' she asked.

He held her look for a moment before he let out a long breath. 'I used to look up to him when I was a young child,' he said. 'I wanted to be just like him when I grew up: successful and wealthy. But as I got older I started to see that, like most people, he had a dark side. He was driven by his emotions. He was selfish and at times outrageously ruthless in getting what he wanted. He exploited the love my mother felt for him. I don't think he ever truly loved her. I think he only married her because he knew she would never challenge him. She would just accept whatever he did without question. She could've left him over his affair with your mother but she didn't. She stayed until the bitter end.'

'Sounds like your father didn't want you to

make the same mistake in your choice of a bride, don't you think?' Sienna asked.

His gaze narrowed. 'What do you mean?'

'Perfect Portia,' she said. 'The wife who would never do or say the wrong thing. The wife who would meekly turn a blind eye when her handsome, charming, virile husband took up with someone else every now and again. That was the sort of marriage you had planned, was it not?'

His frown closed the space between his brows. 'You don't know what the hell you're talking about.'

'Don't I?' she asked with an arch of one brow.

He threw her an irritated look as he wrenched open the door. 'I've changed my mind about dinner,' he said. 'I'm going back to the office. I'll see you when I see you.'

Andreas came home the following evening to find Sienna wasn't home. The villa felt completely different without her in it. The air didn't have that intoxicating trace of her perfume lingering in it, and the scatter cushions on the sofas were all neatly propped in place. There were no half empty cups or glasses littered about, and the television wasn't blaring with some inane reality show or the sound system shuddering with noise that he wouldn't even go as far as calling music.

It was quiet and peaceful, ordered and neat, but sterile.

A bit like his life.

He quickly dismissed the thought and snatched up his phone and rapidly dialled her number. 'Where are you?' he asked as soon as she answered.

'I'm on my way back now,' she said. 'I'm about ten minutes away.'

'Back from where?'

'I've been…erm…at the doctor's,' she said.

His heart gave a sudden lurch. 'The doctor?' he said. 'Why? What's wrong? Are you sick?'

'Not really…'

He heard the hesitancy in her tone. 'What's going on?' he asked.

'I had a bit of an accident,' she said. 'I had to have a couple of stitches in my hand. Nothing serious, however.'

'An accident?' His heart jerked again. 'What happened? Are you all right?'

'I'm fine but you have to promise you won't get rid of Scraps.'

Andreas frowned as he clutched the phone until his knuckles whitened. 'Did that mongrel attack you?'

'It was my fault,' she said. 'I tried to get too close to him. I tried to put some ointment on his sore leg but he wouldn't let me. He snapped at me in pain, not spite.'

'I told you to keep away from that dog,' Andreas said. 'Are you all right to drive? Why didn't you get Franco to take you? Pull over and I'll come and get you. Where are you?'

'Stop fussing, Andreas,' she said. 'You're really starting to scare me. You sound just like a doting husband.'

Andreas drew in a sharp breath and strode over to the windows to scan the driveway of the estate to see if he could see her in the distance. 'That's an expensive and very powerful car you're driving,' he said. 'It needs two hands on the wheel, not one.'

'I won't hurt your precious car,' she said and hung up on him.

Sienna pulled up in front of the villa but didn't even get time to turn the engine off before Andreas had the driver's door open.

'You silly little fool,' he railed at her as he helped her out. 'Why didn't you call me as soon as it happened?'

'I didn't want you to overreact,' she said. 'It's just a scratch.'

He gently picked up her thickly bandaged hand. 'How many stitches?' he asked.

Sienna considered fibbing but decided against it. 'Five,' she mumbled.

'Five?' His eyes flared in alarm. 'That's not a scratch. You could have lost a finger or even your hand.'

'Well, I didn't so everything's all right, isn't it?' she said.

'That dog has to go,' he said trenchantly. 'I will see that Franco destroys it first thing in the morning. And if he won't do it, then I'll do it myself.'

Sienna glared at him as she cradled her hand against her stomach. 'You do that and I swear to God I'll never speak to you again.'

His hazel eyes collided with hers. 'Why are you so determined to rescue a dog that clearly doesn't want to be rescued?' he asked.

She raised her chin at him. 'He does want to be rescued,' she said. 'He just doesn't know who to trust. He'll get there in the end. I just have to be patient.'

Andreas let out a curt swear word as he cupped her by the elbow to lead her into the villa. 'You're going to give me a heart attack one day, *ma petite*,' he said. 'I didn't realise one small woman could cause such chaos.'

Sienna threw him a pert look. 'Just as

well I won't be around any longer than a few months, isn't it?' she said. 'Once this is over you can settle back into your boringly ordered life and forget all about me.'

He shouldered open the heavy front door of the villa as she stalked past. 'I can hardly wait,' he muttered darkly.

CHAPTER TEN

SIENNA woke during the night and had trouble going back to sleep as the local anaesthetic had worn off. The painkillers the doctor had given her were still in her handbag in the car. With all the fuss Andreas had made, she had forgotten to bring it with her into the villa. She tossed off the covers and padded downstairs, turning on the minimum of lights as she went.

She walked past Andreas's study and saw the thin line of light shining from beneath the door. She heard the tapping of his computer keyboard and the squeak of leather as he shifted in his chair. There was a pause in the tapping as she heard him mutter a very rude word, and then the tapping resumed.

She tiptoed past in her bare feet, but one of the floorboards protested volubly and suddenly Andreas's study door was flung open and he stood there towering over her. 'What are you doing?' he said.

'I'm going out to the car.'

His brows slammed together over his eyes. 'Whatever for?'

'I forgot to bring in my bag,' she said. 'The painkillers the doctor gave me are inside it.'

'Why didn't you ask me to get it for you?'

'I didn't think of it till now.'

'Go back upstairs,' he said, rubbing a hand over his weary-looking features. 'I'll bring it up to you.'

Sienna went back to her room and sat propped up against the pillows. Within a few minutes Andreas came in, carrying her bag as well as a glass of water. She took the pills and he set the glass on the bedside table.

'Does it hurt much?' he asked.

'A little,' Sienna said. 'Just a dull throb.'

A little silence passed.

Sienna felt the drumbeat of her heart as his gaze meshed with hers. One of his hands was resting on the bed within a hair's breadth of hers. She felt the magnetic pull of his body, the sensual tug on her flesh, as if all of the organs and cells inside her body wanted to shift to be perfectly aligned with his.

His thumb moved just a fraction and stroked against the little finger of her undamaged hand. It was such a tiny touch and yet it made a tumultuous storm of feeling erupt inside her. Her skin tingled all the way up her arm. Her heart picked up speed and her insides flexed and coiled with unbridled need.

His hooded gaze slipped to her mouth. It felt as if he had physically kissed her. Her lips burned and fizzed and she had to sweep her tongue out over them to dampen down the sensation.

He raised a hand to her face, his touch so gentle it felt as if he were wearing kid gloves. He traced the pad of his finger over the cushion of her bottom lip. It was such an achingly intimate caress—the moisture of her lips and the dryness of his fingertip meeting in an erotic moment that stirred something deeply primal in the core of her being.

'I want you,' Sienna said on a whisper of sound.

Andreas's eyes locked on hers, dark, intense and serious. 'Is that the painkillers talking or you?' he asked.

'It's me,' she said, touching her hand to the stubbly skin of his jaw. 'I want you to make love to me.'

He covered her hand with his and, lifting it from his face, pressed a kiss to the middle of her palm, his tongue moving against the sensitive flesh in an erotic stroke that sent her senses into a tailspin. 'I want you too,' he said. 'It's driving me crazy. *You've* been driving me crazy, do you know that?'

Sienna shivered as he leaned in to kiss the skin of her neck just below her ear. 'We're both a little crazy, don't you think?' she said. 'Hating each other and yet wanting each other.'

His mouth brushed over hers, a light-as-air, teasing kiss that made her want to scream out loud for more. 'Total craziness, that's what it is,' he said, sliding one of his hands underneath the curtain of her hair as he gently drew her closer.

Sienna closed her eyes as his mouth came back down on hers. His lips moved with gentle urgency against hers. The undercurrent of lust that flowed between them made her blood race like high-octane fuel through her veins. Every thudding heartbeat made her longing for him rise to a feverish level. She could feel it building inside her body. A tug and release sensation that resided deep in her womb, making her hot and moist and restless for the full possession of his body.

His tongue commanded entry to her mouth and with a soft sigh of pleasure she opened to him. He played with her tongue, dancing with it, cavorting and teasing it into submission.

Electric shocks arced down her spine when his hand moved to cover her breast. The barrier of her thin nightwear was no barrier at all. If anything, the movement of the fine fabric against her nipple intensified the sensation. But then he pushed the fabric aside and took her nipple and areola in his mouth. It was an explosion of feeling that made her flesh sizzle and shiver with delight. His tongue teased her nipple by rolling over it and circling it, making all the tiny super-sensitive nerves dance in excitement. He uncovered her other breast and subjected it to a similar heart-stopping sensual assault, making her breathing and heart rate go into a frenzied mismatched rhythm.

His mouth came back to her as he gently eased her back on the bed, his weight supported by one of his elbows. 'Let's get rid of this, shall we?' he said, peeling away her nightwear.

Sienna shucked herself out of it, feeling strangely at ease with him without the covering of her clothes. His gaze devoured her hungrily. It made her flesh sing with delight as his eyes took in every curve and contour of her body.

'You're incredibly beautiful,' he said, sliding a hand down over the jut of her hipbone. 'So slender and your skin is like silk.'

'I want to touch your skin,' Sienna said, starting to work on the buttons of his shirt, but she didn't get very far with only one hand.

'Hold that thought,' he said. He lifted himself off the bed and stood there, looking down at her as he undid each button of his shirt, shrugging it off his shoulders before unfastening the waistband of his trousers.

Sienna's eyes followed his every movement with breathless anticipation. Seeing him totally naked for the first time made her breath stall like a misfiring engine. He was all strongly corded muscles and lean and tanned planes. Masculine hair was lightly sprinkled over his chest in a T shape, arrowing down to his groin, where his erection jutted boldly.

He fished a condom out of his wallet and joined her on the bed again. 'Are you sure about this?' he asked. 'It's not too late to stop. I don't want to hurt your hand.'

'It *is* too late, and I've forgotten all about my hand,' Sienna said. 'I want this. I want you.'

His mouth came down and sealed hers with a long passionate kiss that set her flesh alight. He took his time caressing every inch of her body, making her aware of herself in a way she had never been before. She hadn't realised the pleasure spots she possessed. She hadn't known how delicious it felt to have his mouth on the undersides of her breasts, or the way it felt to have his hands stroke the silky skin of her inner thighs. She hadn't known how it would feel to have him gently separate her feminine folds with his fingers and then with the stroke and flicker of his tongue. Her body responded with a sensual energy that took her completely by surprise. It was like a giant wave of sensation that she could not stop even if she tried. It snatched her up in its powerful surge of momentum, tossed her about and flung her out the other side, spent, limbless, breathless and dazed.

Sienna blinked her eyes open and looked at Andreas. 'Wow…' she said.

His hazel eyes glittered. 'It gets better.'

'You can top that?' she said with an incredulous look.

He gave her a smile that made her insides quiver all over again. 'I'll take it slowly,' he said. 'You're tiny and I don't want to hurt you. Just relax, try not to clamp up. You're meant to stretch to accommodate me.'

Sienna sighed with pleasure as he positioned himself so as not to crush her with his weight. She loved the feel of his hair-roughened thighs and the way his hands were so gentle, almost worshipful, as they caressed her. Tasting the feminine essence of her body on his mouth was a new experience, but a totally erotic one. He kissed her lingeringly while his fingers played with her, making sure she was moist and relaxed before he eased into her slowly, pausing as her body got used to his thickness, before going deeper. She felt her inner walls wrap around him; the sensation of him moving inside her made her spine instantly melt. She moved against him experimentally and her belly somersaulted as she heard him give a deep groan of pleasure. 'Am I wowing you?' she asked, sliding her uninjured hand up and down his strongly muscled back.

He swept a strand of her hair away from her face with a tender movement of his hand. 'Most definitely,' he said and, with a spasm of pleasure passing over his face, he took her with him to paradise.

Andreas lay on his side, watching as Sienna slept. She was curled up on her side facing him, her little bandaged hand resting in the space between them. Her hair was a tousled cloud over the pillow. The scent of her was on his skin, the taste of her both sweet and salty on his tongue.

He had made love many times with many women. It was a physical union that he enjoyed. But somehow, making love with Sienna was something else, something infinitely more pleasurable, more deeply satisfying—a mind-blowing experience that touched him where no one else had been able to reach before.

But then she constantly surprised him. That was part of her alluring charm. He never knew what to expect from her. She was totally, and yet somehow delightfully, unpredictable.

She suddenly opened her eyes and gave him one of her breath-snatching smiles. 'I had this amazing dream,' she said. 'This amazingly gorgeous-looking and disgustingly rich guy made love to me. I hate his guts in real life, but in my dream we made magic together. Wasn't that a weird dream?'

Andreas smiled crookedly as he stroked a lazy finger down her cheek. 'Are you sure you hate him so much in real life?' he asked.

She pretended to think about it. 'Mmm, maybe not as much as I did before, but I'm not in love with him or anything.'

'So what's the plan?' he asked. 'A short affair to get him out of your system?'

She tiptoed her fingers up his sternum, making his heart leap like a mad thing behind the cage of his ribs. 'That's the plan,' she said, meshing her gaze with his. 'Five months, give or take a day or two, ought to do it, don't you think?'

Andreas studied her soft plump mouth for a moment. 'What if the amazingly gorgeous-looking, disgustingly rich guy wanted you to stay a little longer?' he asked.

Her grey-blue eyes stilled for a moment. Then she blinked and asked, 'Why would he want that?'

He slowly coiled a strand of her silver-blonde hair around his index finger. 'Maybe he likes having you around to mess up his ordered life,' he said.

She gave a little gurgle of laughter. 'I can't quite see it, somehow,' she said, doing that sexy little tiptoe thing again. 'We'd drive each other nuts.'

Andreas felt an arrow of lust stake him in the groin when her fingers suddenly changed direction, step by exquisite step, as they made their way down to dance tantalisingly over his erection. He snatched in a breath when she boldly circled him with her hand, her soft skin like a silky glove.

She gave him a sultry little smile and bent her head to him, her hair tickling his abdomen and thighs, as she stroked her tongue over his engorged flesh. He groaned out loud as she licked him like a shy, tentative kitten. But then she suddenly turned into a wild rampaging tigress and consumed him whole. Shudders of delight rocked through him as she fed off him hungrily.

He tried to pull away but she pressed him back down with a determined hand. 'Stay,' she said.

'You don't have to do this,' he said, fighting for control.

'You did it to me.'

'That was different,' he said, breathing raggedly.

'"All's fair in love and war",' she said in a sing-song voice.

'So which is this?' he asked. 'Love or war?'

She gathered her hair in one hand before curling it over one shoulder, her eyes glinting with mischief and daring. 'This is war,' she said, and then lowered her mouth and claimed victory.

CHAPTER ELEVEN

In the weeks leading up to her twin's wedding Sienna settled into Andreas's life as if she had always been in it. They didn't discuss the future by tacit agreement, although their affair was as blisteringly hot as ever. She had wondered if Andreas's ardour would cool over time but it hadn't any more than hers had. She had been constantly surprised by her body's capacity for pleasure. His mix of tenderness and daring as a lover repeatedly took her breath away. He would only have to look at her a certain way and she would shudder in anticipated pleasure. She had become more adventurous as her confidence grew. She delighted in catching him off guard, seducing him when he least expected it.

He had been generous to her in showering her with gifts. He had bought her a sophisticated camera and a computer of her own to store her files of pictures. He had encouraged her to have copies professionally printed and had even hung some framed ones in his office in Florence.

Sienna wondered if they would still be hanging there when their marriage came to its inevitable end.

The other project Andreas had helped her with was Scraps. With careful handling and patience, the dog was now totally at ease around them. Andreas drew the line at having the dog inside the villa, but Sienna was content that Scraps was at least healthy and happy and comfortable with the staff as well as her and Andreas.

For once in her life the press left her alone. They seemed to have accepted that she and Andreas were a happily married couple and, apart from an occasional snap of them having dinner or attending a function together, there was no hint of scandal or anything untoward.

Sienna knew it wouldn't last but she tried not to think about it. She was becoming very good at not thinking about things that troubled her. Denial had become her closest companion. As soon as a worrying or wayward thought entered her head she would immediately dismiss it, like her feelings for Andreas, for instance. She absolutely refused to think beyond the fact that she no longer hated him.

What she actually felt for him was locked behind a door inside her head marked private and off-limits.

She just didn't want to go there.

As to what Andreas felt about her, she knew was equally dangerous to examine too closely. He had a goal in mind and within a few rapidly passing months he would achieve it. He would be able to claim his inheritance and move on with his life. She didn't like to presume she would continue to be a part of it.

He never spoke of his feelings. He was attentive and affectionate, and even teasing and playful at times, but occasionally she would catch him looking at her with a frown pulling at his brow. It was as if he wasn't quite sure what to do with her. She suspected she delighted and frustrated him in equal measure.

One such time was a couple of days before Sienna was due to leave for Rome to help her sister prepare for her wedding. Andreas came into the bedroom they shared just as Sienna was sorting out what to take with her. She had been determined to take a leaf from his book and become better organised. She had planned to be packed well and truly in advance—there would no longer be any last minute mad grabs or flying off without packing appropriately. The bed was strewn with clothes and the floor with shoes, but that was all under control, or it would have been if he hadn't come home earlier than she had expected. 'Hi,' she said with a bright smile. 'You're home early.'

His brooding frown looked as if it had been stitched to his brow. 'Do you have to take everything out of the wardrobe every time you get dressed?' he asked.

Sienna lifted her chin, more than a little stung by his surly mood. 'I'm packing.'

A muscle jerked at the side of his mouth. 'What?'

'I'm leaving for Rome, remember?' she said, turning to fling a pair of jeans on to the not-taking-this pile on the floor. 'I'm going to my sister's wedding. I told you about it, not that you probably listened. Of course, it's entirely up to you whether you come or not. No one is pressuring you. I can imagine going to a real wedding where the couple actually love each other will be quite an eye-opener for you.'

'What the hell is that supposed to mean?' he asked.

'Figure it out for yourself,' she said as she pushed past him to fetch a suitcase.

He shackled one of her wrists with his

hand, turning her round to face him. 'What's got into you?' he asked.

'What's got into *me*?' Sienna asked. 'You're the one who came home like a bear with a thorn in his paw.' She shoved at his chest with her free hand. 'Take your hands off me.'

A burning gleam entered his hazel gaze as it collided with hers. 'You wanted my hands on you twice last night and this morning,' he said. 'I've been getting shivers all day just thinking about what you did to me in the shower.'

She threw him a caustic glare that belied her quivering insides. 'Well, I don't want them on me now.'

He tugged her closer, his pelvis hard against hers, his desire warring with her will. 'Prove it,' he said.

'I don't have to prove anything,' she said, giving him another shove, but it was like trying to shift a skyscraper.

He put a hand at the base of her spine, holding her to the hardened probe of his erection. 'One kiss and I'll let you go,' he said.

'All right,' Sienna said, determined to show him she could resist him. She would rise to the challenge the same way she dealt with all of her traitorous thoughts. She would block it from her mind. 'Give me your best, Rich Boy.'

His mouth came down but, instead of completely covering hers, his lips teased the side of her mouth, making every nerve twitch and writhe in rapture. She fought against the desire to turn her head that tiny fraction so her mouth was right under his. She scrunched her eyes closed and tried to ignore the way her body was responding to his as if on automatic. Her spine loosened as he shifted his attention to the other side of her mouth. His stubble caught on her skin, sending a lightning bolt of desire to her core.

'You're cheating,' she said, a little shocked at how breathless she sounded.

'How am I cheating?' he asked, moving up to suck on her earlobe.

Sienna shivered. 'You said one kiss, but you haven't even kissed me.'

'I'm working my way up to it,' he said, coming back to that incredibly sensitive corner of her mouth where her top lip joined her bottom one.

She let out a wobbly breath as his tongue came out to stroke along the partially open seam of her mouth. He still hadn't pressed his lips to hers and yet she was thrumming like a tuning fork struck against a hard object.

Finally she could stand it no longer. She grabbed at his head with her hands, digging her fingers into his scalp as she pressed her mouth to his. He took immediate control by going in search of her tongue, the sensual and commanding thrust of his destroying any hope of her resisting him. She slammed her body up against his, rubbing herself against his arousal, delighting in the crackling sexual energy that fired between them at the intimate contact.

He growled against her mouth as he walked her backwards to the clothes-strewn bed. 'Get your clothes off.'

'Off the bed or off me?' she asked, tearing at his shirt, popping buttons with scant disregard for the designer label it bore.

'Let's start with you,' he said, pulling off her T-shirt as if it were nothing more than tissue paper.

Sienna landed on the mattress with a gasp as he came down on top of her. Somehow her jeans and knickers had met the same fate as her T-shirt. She was naked and sizzling with need as he parted her, thrusting into her with a groan of primal pleasure that made the skin on her arms come up in a fine sandpaper of goose bumps.

He set a rhythm that was breathtakingly fast, his strongly muscled body pumping into hers with raw urgency until she was screaming out loud her release. She wrapped her legs around his waist, desperate to hold on to the exquisite sensations for as long as she could. She sobbed as the final waves coursed through her. She had never felt such exhilarating pleasure. It racked her body with its aftershocks just as his release burst out of him. She felt every shuddering pulse of his body as he spilled. She felt the way the muscles of his back and shoulders finally relaxed under the soothing stroke of her hands.

In that quiet moment of the aftermath, she felt the carapace of her closely guarded heart fall away as if chipped at by a sharpened chisel.

It terrified her.

She could not allow this to happen.

She had to squash it before it took hold.

'Get off me,' she said, pushing against him.

Andreas frowned as he moved to let her get up. 'What's wrong, *ma petite*?'

Sienna shoved her hair back from her face. 'Why do you always switch languages?' she asked irritably. 'It totally confuses me.'

'You understand both Italian and French,' he said. 'It doesn't confuse you at all.'

'I *am* confused,' she said, snatching up a wrap to cover her nakedness.

He rose from the bed and came over to

where she was standing with her back towards him. He put his hands on her shoulders, his breath skating past her ear as he drew her back towards him. 'What's confusing you, *cara*?' he asked.

Sienna turned to face him. 'I'm sorry,' she said, letting her shoulders go down in a slump. 'I think I'm letting my sister's wedding get to me. It's so…so starkly different from ours.'

His eyes searched hers. 'And that's a problem for you?'

She shifted her gaze from his. 'No,' she said, fiddling with a dress on the bed that was now in desperate need of an iron. 'Why should it be? It's not the same thing at all. We're not in love or planning a future together. We both want what we can get out of this arrangement. This little affair we've got going is all well and good for now, but I don't want to be tied to you in the long term any more than you want to be tied to me.'

A long silence ticked past, measured by the rustling of her increasingly haphazard sorting.

'Do you want some help packing?' Andreas asked. 'It looks like you need it.'

Sienna turned and faced him again. 'I can do it by myself,' she said. 'I think it's time I learned how to sort out the mess of my own making.'

'This is not your mess,' he said, frowning as he raked his hair with his fingers. 'This is my father's.'

'Is it?' she asked, giving him a world-weary look. 'Is it really?'

He held her gaze for a long moment. 'I suspect my father wanted to teach me a lesson,' he said. 'He wanted me to understand how hard it is to choose between what I think I want and what I really need.'

'So have you figured it out yet?' she asked.

He continued to hold her gaze. 'I already know what I want,' he said. 'I'm not sure, however, that it's what I need.'

'And what is it that you want, Andreas?' she asked. 'More money? More fame and notoriety?'

He took her by the upper arms and pulled her close, making her heart beat triple time as she felt his body stirring against her belly. 'I think you already know the answer to that,' he said and pressed his mouth down firmly on hers.

CHAPTER TWELVE

'You look absolutely amazing,' Sienna said as she made one last adjustment to Gisele's veil. 'Emilio is going to be speechless when he sees you.'

Gisele smiled as she squeezed Sienna's hands in hers. 'I think Andreas is going to have a similar reaction when he sees you,' she said. 'You look stunning.'

'Thanks...' Sienna slipped her hands out of Gisele's and moved to the dressing table so she could do a last minute touch-up of her make-up before Hilary, Gisele's mother, came back from the suite next door where the hairdresser was styling her hair. With all the bustle of getting ready, it was the first time Sienna had been alone with her sister.

'Is everything all right?' Gisele asked.

Sienna met her twin's grey-blue gaze in the mirror. It still startled her sometimes to see an identical replica of herself standing there.

They were so physically alike it was uncanny, and yet they were so different. 'I'm fine,' she said, forcing a bright smile to her lips.

Gisele came over and put a gentle hand on Sienna's bare shoulder. 'You and Andreas are happy together, aren't you?' she asked. 'It was such a whirlwind courtship, I just wondered if—'

'Of course we're happy,' Sienna said, dipping the lipstick brush in a pot of lip-gloss. 'We're just peachy.'

'You don't have any regrets about having such a small wedding?' Gisele asked.

Sienna's hand trembled slightly as she painted her lips with the lipgloss. 'No, why should I?'

Gisele caught her gaze in the mirror. 'I saw you looking at me when Mum was helping me into my dress,' she said. 'You had such a sad look on your face. I realised then how difficult it must have been for you, getting married without your mother to help you. Is that why you kept things so simple?'

Sienna put the lip brush down with a little clatter on the dressing table. 'I'm not like you, Gisele,' she lied. 'A big wedding has never interested me. For one thing, I'd be rubbish at organising it. I'd probably forget to invite someone terribly important or not order the right colour flowers. Anyway, can you see me wearing white? I wouldn't make it to the church without spilling something on it or tripping over the train or something.'

Gisele smiled and tucked a wayward strand of Sienna's hair back into the elegant style the hairdresser had arranged earlier. 'You're good for Andreas,' she said, putting her hands on Sienna's shoulders and meeting her gaze in the mirror once more. 'I could tell from last night's dinner that he has a tendency to be a little formal and distant. It probably comes from his wealthy background. He doesn't feel comfortable letting people get too close until he works out whether he can trust them or not. I see the way he looks at you. It was as if he can't quite believe his luck to have found someone who loves him for who he is, not for what he can provide.'

Sienna reached for the bronzer brush, even though she really didn't need it given that her cheeks were doing a perfectly fine job of blushing all by themselves. 'He is lucky to have me,' she said. 'We're lucky to have each other.' *Even if it's only for another few months*, she thought.

'He'll make a wonderful father,' Gisele said. 'Have you talked about when you'll start a family?'

Sienna averted her gaze. 'I'm not…He's not…We're not…ready…'

Gisele smiled. 'It's just I have some news for you,' she said. 'I wondered if that was why you and Andreas married in such a rush. I got all excited. I thought it'd be so cool if we were pregnant together.'

Sienna swung around on the stool so quickly her head spun. 'You're pregnant?' she said.

'Yes,' Gisele said, beaming radiantly. 'Emilio is beside himself with pride. We haven't told anyone, other than Mum. I wanted you to be one of the first to know. We're having twins.'

'Twins!' Sienna grabbed Gisele's hands, desperately trying to ignore the sudden pang of envy that seized her. It was wrong of her to feel jealous. It was hideous of her. It was self-ish. She wasn't the one who had longed for a family since she was a young girl. Sienna had no idea of what to do with a baby. She hadn't even held one in her arms.

What right did she have to wonder what it would be like to carry a pregnancy to full term? To feel those tiny limbs growing and moving inside her? To hold that precious lit-tle bundle soon after it was born? To smell that sweet innocent smell and stroke that soft fluffy head?

A wave of longing rushed through her. It set off an ache that felt like a weight pressing down on her heart.

There would be no sweet-smelling babies for her. Andreas had already made it clear how unsuitable he thought her as a mother for his children. He had left nothing to chance. Every time they had made love he had used protection.

The ache tightened in her chest like a spanner working on a nut and bolt.

Just as Sienna couldn't imagine having someone else kiss her or make love to her, she couldn't imagine having someone else's baby. She didn't *want* anyone else's baby.

'Do you know if they're identical?' she asked, thinking of those little limbs wrapped around each other like she and Gisele had been.

'Yes,' Gisele said. 'The ultrasound showed they're sharing the same placenta.'

'And what about the sex?' Sienna asked. 'Do you know if they're boys or girls?'

'Boys,' Gisele said, placing a hand on her only very slightly rounded tummy. 'After losing Lily, I never thought I'd be able to face a pregnancy again, but this time I just know it's going to be different. It *feels* different.'

The door of the suite opened and Hilary

came in, looking every inch the stylishly coiffed and very proud mother of the bride. 'Ready, darling?' she said to Gisele. 'Emilio is eagerly awaiting his beautiful bride.'

Sienna handed Gisele the bridal bouquet, forcing an I'm-so-happy-for-you-smile to her lips, while inside her heart felt as if it were being backed over by an earthmover.

She had already forfeited love.

Would she have to forfeit motherhood as well?

Andreas felt his heart do a couple of leap-frogs in his chest as Sienna walked up the aisle ahead of her twin sister. She was wearing a floor-length latte-coloured satin gown with a cream bow tied over her left hip. Her hair was up in an elegant style that gave her a distinctly regal air. She was breathtakingly beautiful, but then, so too was her twin sister.

He tore his eyes away from Sienna to look at Gisele as she floated up the aisle in an ivory satin gown and a stunning veil and di-amond tiara. Before the bridal party dinner last night he had only seen photographs of her in the press. The likeness, even in print, was amazing but meeting her in the flesh had been totally surreal. It was like looking at a mirror image of Sienna.

It occurred to him then, with an unexpected twinge of guilt, that this was what Sienna would have looked like as a proper bride if he had married her under normal circumstances.

Had *she* wanted something like this?

He felt another ferocious fist of guilt grab at his gut.

Didn't most young women dream of having their day as a fairy tale princess?

As the service got underway he watched to see if any of the heartfelt vows that were being exchanged were affecting Sienna. She stood looking at her sister and the handsome groom with a smile on her lips, but Andreas wasn't sure if that glittery moisture in her eyes was from happiness or something else. She looked rather pale, he thought, and once or twice he saw her lick her lips, from nervousness or dryness, he couldn't quite tell.

Andreas was surprised to find the service so moving. He had attended weddings before and, while he had mostly enjoyed them, he had not felt a lump of emotion suddenly stick like a nut halfway down his throat when the groom promised to love and protect his bride.

Emilio Andreoni was clearly a man deeply in love. His voice cracked unashamedly as he slipped the wedding band on Gisele's finger.

Gisele looked up at him with absolute devotion, tears of joy shining in her eyes.

Andreas felt ashamed of how his marriage to Sienna had been such a sterile, businesslike affair. She hadn't looked at him with her eyes full of love. Hers had glittered with hatred. Their clinical, emotionless union made a mockery of one so sacred and deeply poignant as this. How had his life become such a tawdry sideshow alley game of smoke and mirrors?

He caught Sienna's eye across the church. She smiled at him but it was a weak movement of her lips that didn't involve her eyes. She looked away again, focusing her gaze on the bride and groom as they exchanged their first kiss as a married couple.

Andreas wondered if she was thinking of *their* first kiss. Their mouths had never touched until they had exchanged those meaningless vows. He was reminded of the electric shock of that kiss every time he had kissed her since. It was a power surge in his flesh. He could feel it now just thinking about it. His body ached for her. His blood thrummed with it. He had expected the pulse of lust to wane a little by now, but if anything it had increased. Would the five months left of their marriage contract be enough to satisfy him?

* * *

Because she was part of the bridal party, Sienna was separated from Andreas for most of the reception. It made his hunger for her all the more intense. He couldn't wait until the formalities were over so he could stake his claim. His whole body prickled with annoyance when she danced with the best man as part of the bridal waltz routine. Andreas clenched and unclenched his fists under the table as he watched the best man's arms go around her and bring her up close.

Jealousy was a new experience for him. He could not remember ever feeling it before. He bristled with it. It made his teeth grind together. It made his jaw ache. It made his blood boil.

His gaze narrowed. Was Sienna *flirting* with that guy? She was smiling up at him with that dazzling smile of hers. Her left hand was on the guy's shoulder and her right encased in the grasp of his. Her body was moving in time to the music, a slow romantic waltz that had her pelvis brushing against the best man's every now and again as her feet tangled with his.

Andreas strode across the dance floor and laid a firm hand on the best man's shoulder. 'I'd like to dance with my wife,' he said.

The best man dropped his hold on Sienna

and stepped back. 'Sure,' he said with an easy smile. 'She's a fabulous dancer. I have two left feet but she made me dance like a pro.'

Andreas ground his teeth behind his stiff smile. 'She is indeed an expert at executing tricky manoeuvres.'

Sienna's grey-blue gaze collided with his once the best man had gone. 'What the hell are you playing at?' she asked in a hushed voice. 'You interrupted the bridal party waltz, for God's sake.'

Andreas turned her so she wasn't facing the wedding guests. 'I had to step in before you made a complete fool of yourself,' he said. 'You were practically crawling into that guy's skin.'

She glowered up at him. 'I was not!'

He tugged her against him. 'The only man you should be getting up close and personal with is me,' he said. 'We're married, remember?'

'Only for another five months,' she said, challenging him with her haughty gaze. 'After that, I'm free to be with anyone I want and you won't be able to do a thing to stop me.'

He whipped her around as the music changed tempo, his groin alive with want as her slender thighs bumped against his. 'I wouldn't dream of trying,' he said, 'but for now you are my wife and I expect you to act accordingly.'

Her eyes flashed at him like blue lightning. 'I'm not really your wife,' she said. 'This is just an act, a stupid little game of charades. I'm surprised no one has already guessed we're not the real deal. I'm sure Gisele already suspects something.'

'What makes you think that?' Andreas said, holding her close to him as another couple glided past.

'She kept grilling me on why we got married so quickly and why I hadn't gone for a big wedding,' she said, frowning and chewing at her lip as if the conversation had somehow distressed her.

Andreas deftly led her off the dance floor to a secluded area behind a column. He kept his arms around her, his body thrumming with need with her standing thigh to thigh with him. 'Are you disappointed we didn't have a proper wedding?' he asked.

She pulled her chin back against her neck in a gesture of scorn. 'Are you joking? Of course I'm not disappointed. What we have is a sham. It was bad enough lying in front of a celebrant, let alone a priest and a huge congregation. Anyway, it's different for Gisele.

She loves Emilio and he loves her. They have their whole lives to look forward to.'

Andreas held her gaze for a beat or two. A shadow had passed through her eyes and her beautiful white teeth began to nibble at her bottom lip again. He pushed against the soft pillow of her lip with the pad of his fingertip. 'What's wrong?' he asked.

She jerked her head away from his touch. 'Nothing.'

'I know you better than that, *ma petite*. You always do that to your lip when you're brooding or mulling over something.'

She drew in a breath and then let it out on a long exhalation. 'I'm being stupid and sentimental,' she said, slipping out of his hold. 'Weddings do that to me, or at least ones like this.'

'Yes, well, it was certainly a very moving service,' Andreas conceded. 'Anyone can see Emilio and Gisele belong together. I've never seen a more radiant bride.'

'Gisele's pregnant,' she said. 'She's having twins.'

'That's wonderful news,' he said. 'You must be very happy for her.'

'I am…It's just…' She bit her lip again and dropped her eyes from his.

'Just what?' he asked, cupping the side of her face to bring her gaze back in line with his.

Her eyes shimmered for a moment but then she blinked and her gaze cleared. 'Just as well you're using protection,' she said lightly as she slipped out of his hold. 'Can you imagine the snotty nosed little brats we would make? If we had twins, I bet they'd fight like demons from the moment of conception. I'd probably get stretch marks from all the punches and kicks going on inside.'

Andreas felt a primal tug deep and low in his groin. He pictured Sienna ripe with his seed, her body swelling as each week and month passed. He thought of two little baby girls with silver-blonde hair, or two little boys with jet-black hair, or one of each. He imagined seeing them born, holding them in his arms, loving and protecting and providing for them for as long as he drew breath.

He put a brake on his thoughts like a speeding driver trying to avoid a crash.

In a matter of months he would have everything sewn up the way he wanted it. He would have the chateau and Sienna would have her money. He didn't need or want the complication of being tied forever with her. Their passion would burn out. Their marriage had come about for all the wrong reasons.

He would *not* be a slave to lust.

It would burn out.

It *had* to burn out.

'We should get back to the reception,' he said. 'Everyone will be wondering what's happened to us.'

CHAPTER THIRTEEN

IT WAS late by the time they got back to their room at the hotel. Sienna kicked off her shoes and tossed her wrap on to the bed. She felt tired and overwrought. Her emotions had been building to a crescendo all evening. Andreas's brooding silence hadn't helped. He had barely spoken a word to her during the remainder of the reception. He had danced with her but it had felt as if he were just going through the motions, just like their relationship.

Their marriage was a lie.

It was a farce compared to her sister's. It made her feel like a fraud. It made her feel cheap and tainted. How could she have signed up for something so far from what she longed and yearned for?

She couldn't carry on like this, telling lie after lie after lie. How long before Andreas saw through it? How long before everyone saw through it? She would become an object of pity, just like her mother. She would be known as the woman not good enough, not beautiful enough or smart enough to hold her man.

'I'm going out,' Andreas said.

Sienna frowned. 'What? Now? It's almost one in the morning.'

'I feel like some air.'

She shrugged as if she didn't care either way. 'Don't expect me to wait up for you,' she said, pulling the pins from her hair and tossing them on to the dressing table willy-nilly.

A stiff silence passed.

'I have to fly to Washington DC for a few days,' he said. 'I've organised for Franco to collect you in the morning.'

'You don't want me to come with you?' she asked, meeting his gaze in the mirror.

His expression was unreadable. 'I'll be busy with meetings,' he said. 'The businessman I'm doing a collection for wants me to meet a colleague of his.'

Sienna loathed the feeling of being dismissed like a mistress who no longer held the same fascination and appeal. Was this how her mother had felt? Discarded? Betrayed? Unlovable? Worthless?

Her heart contracted as she looked at

Andreas's stony expression. She was not important to him. How could she have let things get to this? She had betrayed every one of her values. He had used her to get what he wanted. He felt secure now she had succumbed to his seduction. After all, he had nothing to lose. If she left him now, he would still get what he wanted, what he had always wanted. He wanted a wretched old pile of bricks and mortar, not her. She had been a silly little fool to imagine otherwise.

She kept her expression cool and collected. 'Aren't you worried about what people will think of us being in separate countries when we've only been married a month?' she asked.

'I have a business to run,' he said. 'I don't want to be distracted when I'm working on such a big contract.'

'Fine,' Sienna said, throwing him a casual look to cover the wrenching pain she was feeling inside. 'I guess I'll see you when I see you.'

He didn't answer but the door closing on his exit was answer enough.

'What do you mean she's not here?' Andreas said when he got back to his villa in Tuscany a week later.

Elena lifted her hands in a don't-blame-me

manner. 'She told me to tell you it's over,' she said. 'She doesn't want to be married to you any more.'

Andreas sucked in a furious breath. 'When did she leave?'

'The day after her sister's wedding,' Elena said. 'I tried to talk her out of it but she was very stubborn about it. She'd made up her mind.'

'Why didn't you call me and tell me this days ago?' he asked.

'She made me promise.'

'You are employed by me, not her,' Andreas railed at her. 'You should have informed me the minute she left.'

Elena gave him an accusing look. 'Maybe you should have called her every day like a loving husband would have done,' she said. 'Maybe then she wouldn't have run away.'

Andreas clawed a hand through his hair. 'Where the hell is she?' he asked.

'She didn't say where she was going,' Elena said. 'I don't think she wants you to know. She left this for you.' She handed him his mother's ring.

Andreas closed his fingers over the ring until it bit into his palm. He had thought he'd had the upper hand by distancing himself for a few days but Sienna had turned the tables on him. Didn't she want the money? If she left him she would automatically default. She wouldn't get a penny. A month ago that would have pleased him no end. Now, all he could think about was getting her to come back.

He reached for his phone and rapid-dialled her but it went straight to voicemail. He shoved his phone back in his pocket and glared at Elena. 'She must have left some clue as to where she was going,' he said. 'Did she take her passport?'

'I think so,' Elena said, sighing heavily. 'Scraps is pining for her. He won't eat. I'm worried about him.'

Andreas gave a scornful grunt as he raked his fingers through his hair. 'Shows how much she cares about him.'

'She loves him,' Elena said.

'If she loved him she'd be here with him, not running off to God knows where,' he said.

'Maybe she doesn't know if he loves her back,' Elena said with a direct look.

Andreas glowered at her. 'Don't you have work to do? Some cushions to straighten or some clothes to fold and iron.'

'*Sì, signor,*' she said, 'but without Signora Ferrante here there is not much for me to do. She makes this place come alive, no?'

* * *

Andreas went out to the barn but Scraps barely lifted his head off his paws. His woebegone eyes followed Andreas's movements as he crouched down in front of him. 'What's this I hear about you not eating?'

The dog let out a mournful little whine.

'She won't answer her phone,' Andreas said, absently scratching behind the dog's tattered ears. 'I've left hundreds of messages. She's doing it deliberately, you know. She wants me to beg her to come back. But I'm not going to do it. If she wants to default, then that's her business. It's not as if I'm going to lose out if she pulls the plug on our relationship. I still get the chateau. That's all I ever wanted in the first place.'

Scraps gave a low growl, his tawny eyes staring unblinkingly at Andreas.

Andreas pulled his hand away and exhaled heavily. 'OK, I know what you're thinking. You're thinking I'm an idiot for lying to myself for so long.' He sent his fingers through his hair and let out another sigh. 'And you'd be right. I don't care about the chateau. I don't want to live there, not unless she's with me. I don't want to live here without her either. The place is so formal and...*tidy*.' He coughed out a humourless laugh. 'I hate the way she leaves her mess everywhere. Do you know she *always* leaves the lid off the toothpaste? It drives me crazy. But I'd give anything to have her with me driving me crazy right now. I don't know where she is or who's she's with.' His gut clenched in anguish and dread. 'I don't know if I can get her back. What am I supposed to do? Crawl on my belly and beg her to come back to me?'

Scraps gave his threadbare tail a wag against the dusty floor, his eyes still staring wisely at Andreas.

'You're right,' Andreas said, sighing heavily again. 'I'm crazy about her. I'm never going to get her out of my system, am I? We're not talking about lust here. It's never been about lust, has it? What was I thinking? She's the best thing that's ever happened to me. I love her.'

He frowned and gave his head a little shake. 'I can't believe I just said that. I don't think I've told anyone that before, apart from my mother, which is totally different. *I love her.*'

He cautiously reached out to ruffle the dog's ears again. 'What if she doesn't love me?' he asked. 'I'm going to look the biggest fool if I gush out what I feel and she just laughs in my face.'

Scraps let out a long doggy sigh and settled his head back down on his paws.

'I'm not going to tell her over the phone or in a text message,' Andreas said with steely determination. 'I'm going to track her down and talk to her face to face. She thinks she can outsmart me but she's wrong.'

He got to his feet and dusted off his hands. 'If you want to come inside I guess I could make an exception just this once,' he said. 'But no jumping up on the sofas and you are absolutely banned from any of the beds, do you understand?'

The little cottage by the sea on South Harris in Scotland was a perfect hideaway. The long, lonely windswept beaches on the island gave Sienna plenty of time to walk and think about her future—her lonely future without Andreas. She had kept her phone on for the first week, hoping he would call or at least text, but he had cut her loose like the trophy wife he had fashioned her into and, even more galling, she had allowed it to happen.

But now was different.

Now it was time for her to rebuild her life, a life that did not include him, a life without love and passion and fulfilment—a wretchedly lonely, miserable life, the opposite of the one her twin sister was living. How could two people so identical in looks have such disparate lives?

She had phoned Gisele, so as to avoid causing her sister any undue worry but she had refused to say where she was. She knew Gisele would immediately tell Andreas. She wasn't ready to talk to him yet. As far as she was concerned, he'd had his chance and he had blown it.

Sienna had since turned her phone off, only checking it once a day for messages. The second week there were literally hundreds of texts and missed calls from him each day. The messages had progressed from calm and polite pleas to get her to call him, to shouting tirades interspersed with colourful obscenities.

She deleted them all, only wishing she could delete all her memories of him so easily.

She lay awake at night as the wind howled against the shore, whipping up the waves like galloping white horses. She spent hours thinking of Andreas, of his touch, the way his hands felt against her skin, the way his mouth felt against hers, the way his body felt as it claimed hers.

Sienna had been on the island almost a fortnight without once setting eye on a newspaper. She had avoided reading anything on the web browser on her phone as well. She didn't want to know what the press were saying about her and Andreas. But while she was walking on Scarista beach that morning she had briefly turned on her phone and found a message from Gisele alerting her to an article that had come out a day or two before regarding the sex tape scandal. Apparently the man involved had given an exclusive interview to a journalist. He had seen the news of Gisele and Emilio's wedding and had obviously thought he could cash in on the situation by giving a no holds barred tell-all interview.

Sienna read the interview with a churning feeling in her stomach. It brought it all back: the shame and disgust she felt at herself. The way the man told it, she had acted like a drunken slut.

Despair clawed at her chest as she stood on the windswept beach. Was there anywhere she could run, far enough away to hide from this? Was this never going to go away?

But then she pressed on the second link Gisele had sent her.

French-Italian tycoon Andreas Ferrante is pressing charges of slander against Eric Hogan over Mr Hogan's claim that

*he slept with Mr Ferrante's wife Sienna
Baker in London two and a half years
ago. The case is likely to be long drawn-
out and expensive but Andreas Ferrante
says he will not stop until his wife's name
is cleared. Police are making further en-
quiries regarding a possible drink spik-
ing charge on Mr Hogan following the
recent revelations of witnesses.*

Sienna's heart was beating so fast she could
barely breathe. She read the article again, her
eyes prickling with tears.

Andreas had stood up for her.

He had publicly defended her. He was
fighting her battle for her, not even counting
the cost in money, let alone the cost to his
fiercely guarded privacy.

Sienna was heading back to the cottage to
pack when a tall, imposing figure came strid-
ing towards her. She knew immediately who
it was. She felt a shiver run over her flesh as
soon as he came into view. The wild wind
was whipping at his sooty black hair and his
unshaven face looked as thunderous as the
brooding sky above.

'You'd better have a damn good reason for
not returning any of my calls,' he ground out.
'Do you have any idea of the trouble you've

caused? I've spent tens of thousands of euros looking high and low for you. Why couldn't you have just told me? Just one phone call or text. God damn it, was that so hard?'

Sienna just stood there looking up at him. Her gaze drank in his features.

He had stood up for her.

'OK, so give me the silent treatment; see if I care,' he said. He shoved his windswept hair back with one of his hands. 'Just answer me one thing. Why did you run away like that?'

'How did you find me?' she asked.

'Gisele told me she thought she heard bagpipes in the background when you called her,' he said. 'That narrowed it down considerably. The rest I left up to a private investigator. Do you have any idea of what the press have been saying?'

Sienna peeled a strand of hair away from her mouth. 'I haven't seen anything in the press until this morning,' she said. 'I'm sorry about the embarrassment I've caused you.'

'I'm not talking about that,' he said, glaring at her fiercely. 'I've taken care of that sleaze ball. He won't be saying anything about you ever again. How could you think I wouldn't be out of my mind with worry over you? Do you realise what a fool you made me look in front of my staff when I turned up there at the villa and you'd already been gone a week?'

'I'm sorry but I didn't want you to talk me out of it,' Sienna said. 'Anyway, you could have called me. I was giving you a dose of your own medicine.'

'You realise you won't get a penny because of this,' he said still glowering at her. 'You defaulted. I get everything.'

'You've always *had* everything, Andreas,' she said. 'The irony is I've spent most of my life envying rich people like you. I wanted it all: the nice houses and the designer clothes, the jewellery and the fabulous holidays. I thought they would make me happy, that they would make me feel a sense of belonging. But I've come to realise possessions and prestige can never make up for what's most important in life. They're nothing when you don't have love.'

His eyes narrowed in anger. 'You think I don't love you?' he said, shouting above the howling wind. 'I've just spent the last fortnight without proper sleep or food. God knows what's happened to my business because I haven't put a foot inside my office or my workshop. And don't get me started on that contract I just forfeited. I've been too busy trying to track you down to do a thing about it. How dare you stand there accusing me of not loving you?'

Sienna swept her tongue over her wind-chapped lips as her heart went pitter-pat. 'You love me?' she said. 'You're not just saying it to save face and get me to come back?'

'I'm saying it because it's true, damn it!' he said. 'I love your madcap sense of hu-mour. I love your mess. I love the way you tamed a flea-bitten mongrel dog that no one else wanted. I love your smile. I love your laugh. I love your cheekiness. I love the way you nearly always have a spark of mischief in your eyes. I love the way you feel in my arms. I love the way you say one thing and mean the total opposite.' He drew in a breath and released it in a whoosh before he added, 'Have I left anything out?'

Sienna gave him a sheepish smile. 'I think you've just about covered it,' she said.

He let out a laugh and grabbed her, hugging her close to his chest, breathing in the salty sea air that had clung to her hair. 'You little minx,' he said. 'I love you so much it hurts.'

She eased back to look up at him. 'Where does it hurt?'

'Here,' he said, placing one of her hands over his heart.

Sienna blinked back tears. 'I've been so

lonely and sad since Gisele and Emilio's wedding. I couldn't live the lie any more. I didn't think it was right. Your father was wrong to set things up the way he did. It was cruel and manipulative.'

'I know, *ma petite*,' he said, gently cupping her face so he could stroke her cheeks with his thumbs. 'I felt like that too. Seeing the love Emilio has for your sister unnerved me. All of my life I have avoided emotional commitment. I've always set the agenda in my relationships. But with you it was different. I couldn't control what I felt. I refused to confront it. I don't think I really understood how much I loved you until I saw the way Scraps behaved after you left.'

'Is he OK?' Sienna asked. 'I cried like a baby when I left him. My eyes were red and swollen for days.'

Andreas smiled at her. 'He's decided that the barn is no longer suitable accommodation,' he said. 'He's taken up residence in the villa. He has a particular penchant for lying on the sofa watching mind-numbing reality TV shows.'

Sienna smiled back as she looped her arms around his neck. 'That's my boy,' she said. 'I always knew he could be tamed. I just had to be patient.'

Andreas held her close against him. 'I want us to have a proper wedding. I want you to wear one of those fairy tale dresses with a big floating veil, and even glass slippers on your feet if you want. Whatever you want, just tell me and you shall have it.'

Sienna let out a sigh of contentment as she gazed into his hazel eyes. 'What more could I want than you?' she said.

'What about babies?' he said, his expression sobering for a moment. 'You said you didn't want children.'

'Now that you mention it, maybe a baby or two would be nice,' she said.

He kissed the end of her nose. 'I quite fancy the idea of you being pregnant,' he said. 'I think we should get working on that right away. What do you say?'

'Sounds like a plan.'

He held her aloft for a moment. 'Do you realise you haven't actually told me you love me?' he said. 'Here I am shouting it from one end of the beach to the other but you haven't said it back.'

'I love you,' Sienna said, smiling up at him radiantly. 'I love you with all my heart. I think I've always loved you, even when I hated you. Does that make sense?'

He gave her an indulgent smile. 'From you,

my adorable little scatterbrain, it makes absolutely perfect sense,' he said and covered her mouth with his.

* * * * *